PUBLISHER/EDITOR
K. Allen Wood

CONTRIBUTING EDITORS
John Boden
Mercedes M. Yardley
Tom Bordonaro

COPY EDITOR
Sarah Gomes

LAYOUT/DESIGN
K. Allen Wood

COVER DESIGN
Mikio Murakami

Established in 2009
www.shocktotem.com

ISSN 1944-110X

Printed in the United States of America.

Notes from the Editor's Desk

Welcome to issue #7!

This issue marks a new era for Shock Totem Publications. Shortly before our last issue was released, **Nick Contor** chose to step away from Shock Totem and focus his life on different things. Along with **John Boden**, he'd been with us since day one. We wish him well on his journeys, but he is missed.

As a fitting tribute, this issue contains Nick's final contribution to *Shock Totem*: a story by the legendary **William F. Nolan**.

In his stead, we have recruited **Tom Bordonaro**, author of the hilarious, gonzo-nutso "Full Dental" from our fourth issue. Tom swings for the fences, and together we have Very Big Things planned. It's about to get interesting...

But let's talk about right now and what you hold in your hands. Our seventh issue.

Color me biased (I am, so I expect you will judge for yourself), but I think we've delivered another wonderful collection of fiction and nonfiction. And by Beelzebubba, these tales have some looooooooooooong titles!

As mentioned, after meeting Nick at KillerCon IV in Las Vegas last September, **William F. Nolan** sent him "The Horror That Et My Pap—and Other Swamp Stuff," a tale the likes of which you have never read before. This was the last story Nick had a hand in accepting. So here's to you, Nick.

Not to be outdone, **S. Clayton Rhodes** delivers the equally long-titled "The Gates of Emile Plimpkin: The Gravedigger's Legacy," a novelette that veritably oozes classic horror. **Damien Angelica Walters** (formerly **Damien Walters Grintalis**), a woman never known to shy away from getting creative with story titles, gives us the heartbreaking "Shall I Whisper to You of Moonlight, of Sorrow, of Pieces of Us?"

As always we're not afraid to put newcomers front and center, and this time we begin with the one-two punch of "Consumption" and "Among the Elephants," by **Victoria Jakes** and **Amberle L. Husbands**, respectively. In "The Long Road," **Kristi DeMeester** leads us to the water's dark edge and tempts us to drink deep, drink long, because we are so very thirsty.

Rounding things out are **Dominik Parisien's** excellent poem, "Smoking, The Old Sergeant Remembers 30 Mins Past Ceasefire," and the creature-feature "Thing In a Bag," by **M. Bennardo**. What's in the bag? Well, you'll just have to read on and find out...

In addition to all the great fiction, we have for you conversations with literary stalwart **Laird Barron** and **Violet LeVoit**. The early 70s are explored in the fifth installment of our horror-in-music serial, "Bloodstains & Blue Suede Shoes." Narrative nonfiction is handled by **Kurt Newton**, and with "The Hook, the Hole, and the Garden," **John Boden** delivers possibly the most heart-wrenching piece of nonfiction we've ever published.

And that pretty much covers the big stuff.

Next month marks the fifth anniversary of when I first decided to publish a magazine. Many of you have been with us since those early days, and we've picked up many more along the way. I cannot thank you enough for sticking with us, and I hope you'll stick around for years to come.

It's been a hell of a ride thus far, and we've got plenty of gas and long roads ahead.

K. Allen Wood
July 1, 2013

Contents

Article
THE HOOK, THE HOLE, AND THE GARDEN

by John Boden

The pre-divorce memories I have of my parents are scattered, a handful of seeds from a quaking hand.

I was around seven, and my little brother two, when our father left. That was how I had always assumed it: Dad left. He got up and went to work one day and never came home. Not home to us, anyway. He wanted a new family and had found one. With two girls the same ages as me and my brother, it felt like we had been replaced. For some reason we had grown stale or broken and my father wanted something fresh.

At that young age, the first pangs of resentment began to sprout. The beginnings of a cold garden, one I would tend for decades.

When we would go to Dad's for our agreed-upon weekends, it was always awkward. I held such disdain for the girls who now called my father, "Dad." Being young affords you a certain lenience or ignorance with the processing of fact. Perception is often skewed to the point of abstract. I think back to the weekends and wish I had known better then. These girls were the mirror twins of us, my brother and me, and it was every bit as awkward for them as it was for us. And I'm sure it had been awkward for our older half-sister, whom we didn't see very often. But being a child, I bottled all those bad feelings and watered the garden with them.

Sometime in early adulthood, I took a notion to write my father a letter, and let him know exactly how I felt about things. Still too young to think straight and still hot-tempered, I penned a vile letter. I told my dad I felt he was a sham and a coward. I told him that when I was a kid I looked at him as a superhero and now he was just a man. It hurt him deeply. And of all the things in my life I wish I could take back, that is surely topmost.

My garden was growing out of control and the plants that resided there were voracious.

Resentment is a lot like a fishhook. It gets in your craw and holds you steady. You can fight and try to pull free, but it will usually just nestle in tighter and bind you fast. Some of us swallow the hooks, some never bite. Most of us, I think, just learn to live with the nagging pull at our throats.

Before I got married, I had begun the long road to mending the relationship with my father. I came to realize the wisdom he had to offer and that what I had always took for complacence and ignorance was more of a genial pride he took in his children. I loved sitting and talking with him for hours, even though I could hardly do so without thinking of the bile I had spewed. I enjoyed his stories of his childhood with my uncles and aunts or the family history he knew so well, and many times I swore that I was going to record these things and preserve them, but I never did. When I would call and we would talk on the phone, I always had so much I wanted to say but couldn't articulate.

My stepmother handled the card sending, birthdays and Christmases. For the longest time she signed the cards from both of them. Then one year, I got a birthday card. Signed *Dad*, in his own handwriting. It was such a simple thing but it meant so much. I saved every card he signed from that point on.

As time marched on, I never visited enough. When I did, it was always warm embraces and lots of talking. His smiling eyes and little ways. I'd give him books I was a part of, books he'd never read but showed off to whomever stopped by. I was his son, and he was proud of all I did. He was that kind of man, exuding an immediate ease with everyone. I wish some of that had been passed on to me.

On Black Friday, November 25, 2011, I came home from work to a message from my sister. "Call Dad and listen to his voice." He was very sick and would not allow her to take him anywhere. I picked up the phone and hit DAD. After a few rings an old man answered. An ancient sounding voice trying to sound like my father. He sounded weak and frail, and through the course of our very brief conversation, a bumper crop of fear and terror sprang to life in my guts. "Oh no," a small voice whispered in my ear. Once I got myself together, I called my brother.

By Sunday, he was in the hospital. I visited him as often I could. He was so small and thin and unlike the man I had seen months prior. My sister told me the diagnosis, one I already knew. Cancer. All over the place. She shoveled no bullshit. She's a nurse, one of the best, and what she said hurt more than anything I had ever heard. We cried, and as a family we grew stronger. I wrote a letter to my father. A deeply honest letter and apologized for all I had said or done when I was younger. I told him how much he meant to me and how much I loved him and how proud I was to be his son.

I took it with me to the hospital but never read it to him. I gave it to my stepmother to read to him later.

By my birthday, Dad was going home. They had made a plan to hopefully start chemo and other treatments as soon as he was able to eat. Dad just wanted people to stop poking at him. He just wanted to go home. He wanted to be in his own house and he wanted buffalo chicken pizza from Pizza Hut.

He got home on Friday and I called and talked to him briefly, then my stepmother for a bit. She said he was tired and that Monday they would go to a nearby hospital to put together his treatment regimen. I told her I would be up to see him early that week.

Later that weekend, they took Dad to the ER. He was admitted and by the time I got to see him, the following Wednesday, he was no longer conscious. I didn't think I would be able to cry anymore. A person has to run out of tears eventually, right? I held his hand and kissed his brow before we left. My stepmother told me she hadn't read his letter yet, but she still had it. I told her it was okay, we can read it to him when he's home.

They sent him home the Thursday before Christmas. I cut out of work early on Friday to be with him and the family. I came back to my own home on Christmas eve to spend it with my wife and sons. Dad would never have wanted me to miss that time with them. After Christmas dinner at home, I drove back up to my father's place. We sat with him all evening. My stepmother slept on the couch, adjacent to his bed. My sister and I sat and listened to the sound of his breathing. It got worse and worse. To this day I can't stand the sound of coffee brewing.

Shortly after 3 a.m., he passed away.

We were all present, his wife and his children. It was heart-crushingly sad, but also very special. One of the few opportunities we are afforded is to allow someone to know how much they are truly loved. I sat in the living room with my siblings and we watched as the funeral director and his crew collected my father and took him away. Nothing can ever be more sobering than that...well, maybe until you help choose a casket. We made it through, hopefully stronger, and while our family grew closer during that very difficult time, we've all kind of strayed back to our respective lives and those connections have worn down.

It's been almost two years and not a day goes by where I do not think of that man, my father. I think of his smile and his eyes and that voice. I want to hear him laugh. I just want to hear him. The hole in our lives is so great, I know it will never be filled.

I used to grapple daily with the thoughts of regret and "If only I had..." I long for a day when I'm strong enough to go to that garden, weed-choked monster that it is, set it ablaze, and baptize myself in that pitiful smoke, and come to grips with the fact the we all have regrets and we all wish we were better, had done more.

Over time the hurt does ease, but just a little. I know I am not alone in these feelings. I'm certain this scenario has played out in many of our lives, maybe even playing out right now. Most of us will face the tragedy of our parents dying. Our children, siblings. The void such loss creates in our souls is not meant to be filled. I think it is meant to be honored and treated with reverence. Love and reverence make for better soil than regret and guilt or resentment.

And that which will bloom there will always be beautiful...

Consumption

by Victoria Jakes

I am suffocating in this summer of desire.

The air is too thick, too heavy, for coveting of this magnitude. It soaks my skin, so I am always slick, always damp, never clean. I will never be clean again.

X leaves in the morning. X is my forever. He kisses me when he says goodbye, then pretends to forget his keys so he can come kiss me again. When I was small, such an act could have occupied an entire afternoon of make-believe with my dolls. Ken just has to kiss Barbie one more time. He can't help himself. How romantic, to be uncontrollable.

Now, I am out of control.

Sometimes, I imagine myself small enough to crawl under X's skin, into his stomach cavity. There I would find safety amidst his organs. A benign tumor of love. When I wrap his arms around me, will him to squeeze me until I cannot breath, it is never enough. I am overwhelmed with his care, but until he engulfs me totally, infinitely, it will never be enough.

~

I meet Y by the ruins of the old hospital. I think the crumbling infrastructure is romantic. Not, like, Paris-in-the-spring romantic, but pain-so-profound-it-lingers-permanently romantic. Y is not particularly sold on the idea. He prefers his beauty untouched by humans, even if our interference has now been reclaimed by the earth. We talk it over for a while. In the end, the ghosts of our world only mean something to Y because they mean something to me.

Y asks about X. Y and X are friends. In some parallel universe, Y and X could be in love. In a bizarro world, where they are not men but humans, Y and X would be lovers. It is a tragedy that our world can be so strange, but never the way I need it to. Y and X never touch. Not drunk. Not in a playful jest. Not in a friendly hug. Their distance speaks more than they know.

I am not so disciplined.

When Y makes me laugh, I touch his arm. Fleeting, or it is supposed to be. I can't anticipate how hot his skin is. It smokes against my fingerprints. If I were to press my body against his, I might combust. I am desperate to be incinerated.

This is not melodramatic. This is how it actually is.

The old buildings whistle with a breeze I cannot feel. The dead watch us as I peel my hand away, as we move apart, as regret pounds down on me until my bones threaten to crumble. In a place like this, the dead recognize sickness. They can see my guilt ruining me.

Y asks me if I am okay. I tell him I am fine.

It was not supposed to be this way.

X is my forever. I know this in the part of my mind still avoiding the crush of need for someone else. I know this in the part of my mind that knows there are no ghosts here. I know this in the part of my mind that insists on sanity.

X will be away for five more days.

~

I am bored without X. I can barely sleep without him. I watch episode after episode of procedural television in an attempt to give structure to my day. Victim, suspect, evidence, twist, suspect, judgment, punishment, repeat. Y calls after the fifth judgment. I am ready to be punished.

Today is less humid, and in turn, I want Y less. We walk in circles around the empty town, shooting the shit about our uncertain futures, our unhappy pasts, and how much we love X.

I picture a sitcom scenario of the three of us living together. It would be all homoerotic jokes and dancing dream sequences and never-ending, will-they-won't-they sexual tension. The laugh track echos in my ears. We can do this, ha ha ha. We can be friends, ha ha ha.

Y goes back to his house for dinner, and I go back to mine. But then he calls, wants to see me again that night. This should be fine, ha ha ha. We had such a normal day, ha ha ha. I really need a friend, ha ha ha.

Maybe it would have been fine, had Y not decided to shave in his hour away from me. I don't know why he did it. His face was scruffy earlier, but now it is smooth, which doesn't matter, except that he's nicked himself on his neck. A perfect droplet of blood formed and dried just below the shadow of his jaw.

The only option for not staring at it would be stabbing my eyes out. I consider it. I must put my mouth on that spot, I must taste and swallow him, I must have him inside me or every essential function of my biological being will forfeit the war against death and I will collapse under this mountain of desperation.

X calls after Y leaves. X is pleased I am making the effort to be friends with Y. I say nothing. X is the only person in the world who bears the weight of my secrets and I cannot give him this one to carry. It will crush him.

I pretend to be the only person this will turn to dust.

~

When I met X, I fell into him with ease. That rare compatibility they don't show on the television because it's kind of boring on screen. In person, it is a revelation. One moment, I was alone. The next, I never had to be alone again. We shelter the same demons, we believe in the same magics, we fuck in three-four time, and climax simultaneously. It is that simple.

When I met Y, I didn't look twice at him. When I met Y a second time, I didn't like him. It took years for us to have a conversation. I even have it written in my journal.

Of X's friends, I find Y the most difficult.

Maybe that was it. The challenge of him. Y surprised me, continues to surprise me, when I know every surprise ending in existence. Y is never dead the whole time, or secretly multiple personality disorder, or a childhood sled. Instead, he is beautiful and masculine and angry, but then, in a shocking twist, he admits to being wrong and laughs at my jokes and is crippled with existential quandary. Y looks like the plainest, vanilla boy ever to please-and-thank-you his way through the world. But inside, Y is strange. In the biggest twist of all, inside, Y is like me.

Y has a girlfriend I never see. I hate that I am jealous of her.

Sometimes I fantasize about desecrating my body for Y. I slice off my scarred skin. I carve away from my hips and stomach and thighs until I am the right shape and size. I open up my skull and present my mind to him as an offering. I would be raw for him.

I am reduced to my physicality. I am nothing but pulsing veins and firing neurons. My body breaks under the drag of his gravity.

Y calls me, waking me up from my afternoon doze. We go walking along the old train tracks in a hot drizzle. There is so much water dispersed in the air that I am saturated with summer. Y is not in a good place today, but he won't tell me why. I am not in a good place, either. We walk in silence.

Y is an imploding star. He sucks me in, collapses me, simplifies me until I am indistinguishable from the earth, muddy with the weather.

He touches me this time, by accident. He's walking along the track like a balance beam and teeters, seizing my hand as if his fall might be infinite. I start like he's made of acid. The only way I will scrape his iron grip from my mind is by amputation. Even then, my phantom limb would obsess over the sensation.

I throw up.

He watches me, too terrified to touch me again.

X calls that night. Y texted him and told him that I was sick. X is worried. X wants to come home. I try not to cry, lest I lose any more of myself to this absurdity.

X is my forever. Forever will not last much longer.

~

I call Y to have an awkward conversation about why we can't be friends, but before I can say anything, he tells me he's outside my house. He wanted to get out of his house, started to wander, and ended up here.

I hate him, briefly. But I've got need itching up my spine, craving burning in my belly, and fifty-billion tons of attraction shackled to my ankles. I am too thirsty for him to hate him.

When I invite him in, he stands too close, then too far, then too close, then too far. His indecision in my living room puts me on edge. I yell at him about nothing, and he yells back about even less, and it's like the room is on fire.

I tell him I cannot endure him.

He says he cannot endure himself.

~

Y and I walk in the woods with inevitability cumbersome on our shoulders. He keeps offering me water from his canteen. I can't take anything from him until I take everything.

The woods are not like the hospital. The spirits here are ancient. They don't judge, they don't care. They were here long before we crawled from the ocean and they will be here long after we sink back into it. Whatever I do here will be consumed by maggots and reborn into tiny, curling greenery. My sin will give the world much needed breath.

Y doesn't speak when I come close, invading his space. He doesn't step back when I am near enough to steal his breath. His eyes flutter shut and his breath stumbles when I strip off his cotton armor, piece by piece. That I am not demolished by lust in that moment is a miracle.

He spreads his legs as if he's done this a thousand times before. He is hard for me, which is sort of a surprise, but he doesn't flinch when he sees my knife, which is a definite surprise. I am so thankful for him. He kisses me, once, and I tell myself it means he is thankful for me too.

He whimpers when I cut into his femoral artery, but stays still.

His life spills forth, a shock of red, and I am quick to contain him with my mouth. He tastes of iron and earth and human. I drink him down, all the way, let his power sprawl through every pathway of my insides and purge me of the beast I have become.

When he grabs my hair I almost break suction to scream, overwhelmed with conclusion. But he holds me there, smashing my nose against the dusting of hair on crease of his thigh. It's not long before his grip becomes weak and I can take no more. He is everywhere inside, thrashing through me, but he is barely there on the ground.

I lay next to him while what remains trickles free into the damp underbrush.

Y becomes the only cold thing in this summer world.

~

X will be home soon. I watch the clock. Y soaked me, his stain dried all over my skin. But I am light for the first time in months. I have devoured what once consumed me. It is a terminal solution.

I won't let X live with what I've done. I shed a few tears then, over everything that should have been. But if I have always been capable of this, if these past few hours are indicative of some true nature lurking inside me, then it is foolish to pretend we could have lived indefinitely without incident. There is no justice here, only victims and punishment.

My single regret is that I could not release my desire the way I now release my guilt. What an insidious, imperfect system, this being of mine. If there was any reason in this world, I would have been incapable of love. But I won't regret loving X. It is impossible to regret loving X.

X is my forever. Forever ends today.

Victoria Jakes is a writer and artist living in New Orleans. She migrated from the bitter cold of Massachusetts last year, and has fallen in love with her new city of graveyards, humidity, and dive bars. Victoria gets paid to play with dogs and sometimes pull poop out of their mouths, but is happiest when she is creating. Comic books, stop motion animations, short films, paintings, and zombie makeup all fall under Victoria's creative pursuits, but writing is her primal calling. She is currently shopping her first novel.

Victoria lives with her man, Nick, and her miniature pit bull, Midna. You can follow Victoria on Twitter at @victoriajakes, but Midna tweets more often at @MidnaThePitPup.

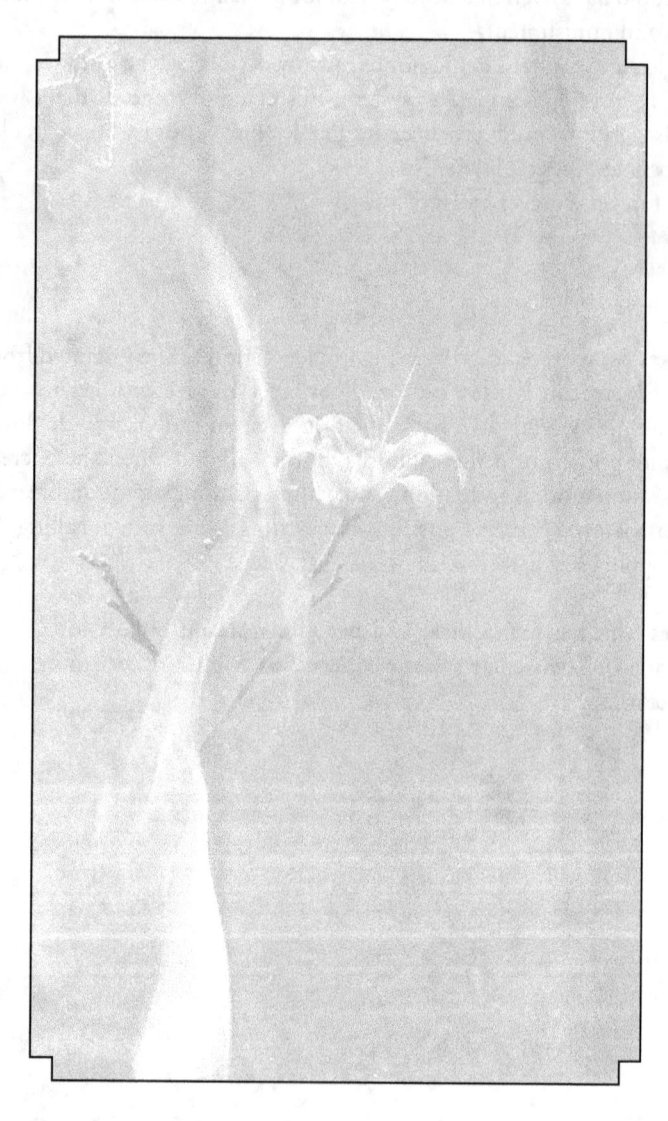

Am⊙ng the Elephants

by Amberle L. Husbands

I'd dreamt of the Elephant Man, every night for the past week, ever since they'd given me the assignment. In my heart, I knew better than to think of Joseph Merrick as the "Elephant Man," but asleep, in my dreams, I couldn't help it. Monday morning came, finally, and I dressed and went to the address they'd given me, to assume my duties as Sarah Bartell's private nurse.

It was the personal, explicit warning that had me frightened. When he awarded me the position, Mr. Krajik had drawn me into his office and closed the door behind us. In all my trips up to the labor offices, I had never once seen that door closed.

"I'll understand," he began, "if you don't feel this s a job you can do."

At first, I was offended. I'd been training for over five years to become a nurse, and thought I'd done pretty well at it, even; head of the class, nearly always. But then Mr. Krajik continued.

"It's mostly her face," he explained. "The deformities in her hands, arms, chest, all of that, aren't any worse than some of the saw mill accidents you no doubt saw in school. But her face... Don't make the mistake that she's blind. She isn't. She'll see you, if you stare at her."

"I wouldn't do that," I protested, still slightly offended.

"You say that now," Mr. Krajik answered, quirking up one eyebrow in gentle, amused sympathy. "If you want the job, it's yours. I just want to know that you're up to it."

I took the assignment, glad for any work. But as the date of our meeting drew closer, the dreams began, and to my shame I found myself dreading the face of Sarah Bartell.

~

I found out, much later, that Sarah and I had been born during the same winter, only a month apart. Still, though, she was already an old woman by the time I made it out of school. She had grown up down south, with an adventuresome mother. Down there—though people were even less understanding—there were more wild, wide-open places to run to and escape them for a little while.

I say she was an old woman mostly because she had never been a little girl. One of the first doctors had told her mother that the girl would only live to be ten or eleven years old, at the most. Sarah heard him, and I think she must have made up her mind to become an old woman in that instant. She ceased to be young, at least.

They traveled, I'd heard, through the girl's childhood. But then her mother had died, and Sarah closed herself up before the world could get too complete a look at her. She haunted her own world, traveling to unknowable hellish regions, I'm certain, without ever even peeking out the window. Only whispers of her, like hideous ghosts, reached us on the outside.

Sarah was twenty-nine, when I went to work for her.

~

Monday morning, I waited in her downstairs parlor, fingers dancing nervously at my sides as the time for me to meet my mistress came and went. I hate to admit it but must: As seven o'clock became seven-fifteen, then seven-thirty, I began hoping that she'd died in the night, relieving me of my duties before they'd begun.

Her house was bigger than I'd expected, but by no means extravagant. It had been a cook who'd brought me in and situated me in the parlor, explaining that Ms. Bartell would see me in the solarium, presently. The place was very similar to my father's house on Elm Street. The main distinguishing features were the heavy curtains still drawn across the front windows, and even these didn't stop the rooms from being flooded with early light.

Finally, I heard a door open and shut, and a young man came down the hall, stopping in the parlor for his hat and a briefcase.

"She won't see me," he said over his shoulder, as if the matter was something I'd be interested in. "One of the best geneticists on the east coast, and *she* won't see me."

I almost blurted out how fortunate he was, betraying myself and my shameful horror. But as he was slamming the front door I heard my name called, and went down the hall into the sun room, to meet the woman face-to-face.

I didn't drop my eyes.

I stared.

But I made sure to smile as I did it, the brightest, bravest smile I could possibly manage. And slowly my terror subsided, creeping away little by little with each stolen glance. She *did* appear blind; only the slightest flickering of wet blackness from two pits, hidden deep within the folds of her face, proved otherwise. Her neck curled away from where it should have connected, thin and bent, and her voice crept out of it tangled and snarled. Her face was mostly immobile. I don't know whether it was physically so or if she had simply trained it not to betray her. But in that first moment, when I didn't drop my eyes, I did see one thing, one emotion. I think, to this day, that it was a flash of fear.

~

I began to see deformity, whenever I closed my eyes. The nightmares didn't go away, though I eventually stopped blaming her for them. In the instant between first sleep and oblivion—long before proper dreams stirred themselves—I would suddenly see horribly mutilated faces, staring back at me from a void. I would see twisted, torn bodies, or parts of them, or starving, mangled animals eating one another. They were just imagines, just visual flashes filling the open gaps of my mind, but each scene gripped me with such intense terror that I would often jump awake stifling a scream, when I'd just nodded off the instant before.

The fear in these images—and I must confess, I believed I was glimpsing Hell, at the time—was unlike anything I'd ever experienced...

But almost immediately upon waking, they would leave me filled with a heavy sadness instead of the fear. I couldn't bear to think of a world where such pain and miserableness existed...and couldn't bear to accept that my own mind would invent such atrocities.

Was that really the stuff that filled my head, I wondered; was *this* really the stuff I was made of? Was pain the language that I thought in?

~

"There's no such thing as Hell," Sarah croaked one day, straining to be nearer to my ear as I held her medication up to those hard, twisted lips. "We've already come through that part...and this world is the reward for whether we performed nobly there...or not."

"How does a person perform nobly in Hell?" I asked her.

"You plant flowers," she hissed. "You feed the birds, while they're burning."

I dared not ask how she believed either one of us had performed, to be awarded our present lives. After all, she'd been given almost two decades of borrowed time, while I was still seeing Hades inside my eyelids.

~

"Do you know what's funny?" she asked another time, after I'd been working in her house for nearly a month.

I waited, leaning close to hear Ms. Bartell's strangled voice, balancing the plastic cup with that day's first round of liquid-mercy on my knee. I knew she lived in horrifying pain, but she was never in a hurry to take her medicine. I could not imagine what this woman could possibly find funny about the world we lived in.

"I've heard all the jokes, or imagined what they must be," she continued. "You know what? My mother really *did* work with elephants... For a zoo, back down south. And they loved her... She took me to meet them, once, after hours. When I was just a girl...I was afraid they'd trample me, think me monstrous...but she said that, to them, I smelled enough like her that they'd love me on sight. And they did! They never batted an eye, they just loved me as my mother's daughter... I wish now I'd spent more time there, with them."

I didn't work for her long, but I was there the morning that she sat back in the sun room and stopped breathing. She'd been planning a trip to Africa—one we both knew would never come to exist in reality. That was okay; the plans were enough. She wanted to stand in an old place, she told me, one that still remembered what the world was like before people walked across it...

Sometimes I wish I'd spent more time among the elephants, too.

Amberle L. Husbands is a writer currently living in middle Georgia. Her short stories have appeared in the **Alchemy Press** *Book of Pulp Heroes*, as well as on the websites *Underground Voices*, *Fear and Trembling*, and *The Cynic Online*. Her first novel, *See Eads City*, was released in October of 2011.

A Tale of True Horror

THE FOUR HORSEMEN OF THE PARKING LOT

by Kurt Newton

The four young men standing in the parking lot didn't look cold. In fact, none of the four wore winter coats even though it was eleven o'clock at night and below freezing outside.

The four stood in a clot in front of a parked car. At the center stood a young man with blond hair. His eyes were closed, his head tilted up toward the night sky. The other three surrounded him, one on each side and one standing in front. The one on the left had his hands placed firmly on the blond man's shoulder and forehead. The one on the right had his hands holding the back of the blond man's neck and cupping his chin. The third, who crouched slightly in front, his head turned toward the pavement, had both hands placed against the blond man's chest. He appeared to be feeling for a heartbeat.

My first thought was the blond man had been skateboarding in the parking lot and had fallen. I don't know why I thought this because the men, though young, were too old and too well-dressed to be skaters. Besides, the small parking lot was gated and private. Only guests of the house were allowed inside.

I kept expecting the blond man to open his eyes, but then I realized all four of the men had their eyes shut. Their lips were also moving, subtly, repetitively. It was then that it occurred to me that the four were in the midst of some kind of prayer. So I turned away.

Maybe they were friends or relatives praying for someone inside the House. After all, the house I was staying in was the Ronald McDonald House in New Haven, Connecticut. No, I wasn't there to get a bite to eat. I was there because my newly born granddaughter was at the hospital nearby, close to death.

~

Two days earlier, the birth of my daughter's baby filled me with pride, dread, and relief. Pride that my daughter hadn't chosen the path of least resistance and opted instead to accept a responsibility that for most teenagers would be a horror. Dread that now there would be an infant in our house, the first in fifteen years, and the normal course of our lives would be disrupted. Relief that the baby was at last here and I would not have that daily reminder of a pregnant, unmarried, teenage daughter walking around the house, and the parental guilt that goes along with that. Maybe my wife and I were somehow bad parents for allowing something like this to happen. Maybe we were too strict. Maybe we weren't strict enough. Maybe we didn't tell our daughter the things she needed to know. Maybe, maybe, maybe. But all that ceased to matter when the baby was born and it was discovered that something wasn't quite right.

Neveah Alicia Ann Newton weighed in at seven pounds three ounces. She looked exactly like my daughter when she was a newborn. Family and friends gathered and we took turns holding her. She wouldn't open her eyes. She was shy, we thought. She also refused to nurse. She preferred instead to be wrapped up tight and to sleep. Instead of crying she cooed like a bird. As we held her, we thought the sounds she made were cute. We joked that because our daughter was so close to her cat, that perhaps Neveah was part feline.

I went home that night believing nothing could possibly be wrong. The hard part was over. My daughter had made it through and a new chapter of her life had begun. My wife stayed at the hospital for our daughter's sake. Just before bedtime, the phone rang. It was my wife. She was in tears. Neveah was having seizures. A CAT scan revealed signs of bleeding on the brain. She might have spinal meningitis. She had been placed on oxygen. She might have brain damage. They were rushing her to Yale-New Haven Children's Hospital as we spoke. She might not survive the night.

Take a breath. Think positive. Helpless, helpless, helpless. For the first time in my life I actually asked God for a little favor. It was a simple request. "God," I said, "please help Neveah. She deserves a shot."

~

Next came the long drive. Bigger hospital, bigger waiting room. One by one we went in to see Neveah. Tubes, tape, monitors, so many machines for such a small person. There was a piece of gauze placed over her eyes. Apparently, the infection in her brain made her sensitive to light—even the light that bleeds through the eyelids. She was stable now. She had stopped seizing. They were able to determine from the spinal fluid that she had contracted strep-B, a common bacteria to us, but life-threatening to infant immune systems. They were treating her with penicillin. An MRI was scheduled for the morning to determine the extent of damage, if any.

That night my wife and I and our daughter went to the Ronald McDonald House to stay for the night, the first of many to come. That night, while getting a late night snack, I saw the four young men outside the kitchen window.

The following morning I woke up early, grabbed my pad, went downstairs, and in the early morning quiet of the House's large sunroom, I began writing this down. The original ending went something like this:

I want this to have a happy ending. I want this to just be a story my daughter will tell Neveah when she's older.

Later that day, I asked the volunteer at the House about the four men in the parking lot. I hadn't seen any of them inside the House. She looked at me and smiled and said, "A lot of strange and miraculous things happen around here. This is truly the house love built."

I smiled back, but at the same time a chill ran up my spine.

Well, that's a lie. It's funny the things we cling to, the stories we tell ourselves when we don't want to face the truth, when we want to avoid that feeling of helplessness. My granddaughter's life was in the balance and here I was writing some kind of sappy spiritual ending to a story not yet finished.

Maybe I wanted the four men to be an apparition, four angels sent by God to help Neveah get the shot she deserves. The shot I petitioned for. It would be cool and kind of scary to believe the universe actually operated that way.

But I'm too much of a skeptic to believe that to be true.

The truth is I did ask the volunteer in the House about the four young men I had seen. I was told that sometimes Yale divinity students stay at the House. I guess that explained what I saw.

The truth is sometimes prayers are answered, sometimes not. The truth is helpless comes with the territory. As do tears. As does death.

And now for the happy ending...

It's been ten days since Neveah entered the children's ICU. Every day she gets better. Subsequent tests have revealed no permanent damage. She must be a fighter. She must be lucky. She must have an angel looking over her shoulder. Pick whichever belief you're most comfortable with.

As I write this she is still at Yale-New Haven. She has another week to go before they release her. She is now breathing and eating on her own. She opens her eyes often and even cries now and then.

Welcome to the world.

Kurt Newton's fiction has appeared in *Weird Tales*, *Dark Discoveries*, *Shroud*, and *Shock Totem*. His novel, *Powerlines*, was recently published by **Gallows Press**. He lives in Connecticut.

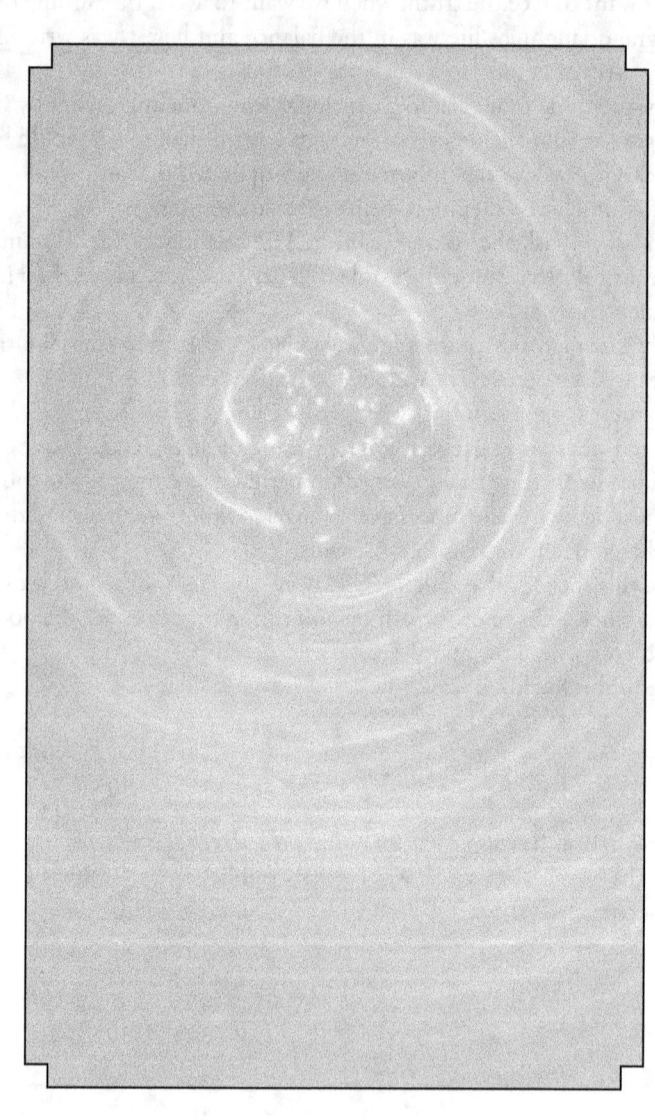

There Is Always Something Worse
A CONVERSATION WITH LAIRD BARRON

by Michael Wehunt

Horror is easy. It's everywhere: on your own street or in grainy images of unrest half the world away. There is little need to seek it out. Reading fictional horror can seem like overkill when the actual world is dripping with it. Sure, horror provides an escape from life just as fantasy and science fiction do. But perhaps unique among fiction genres, horror involves facing those terrible realities, processing them into monsters that can bring deep eddies of understanding...all while never quite looking away from the mirror.

Horror is easy, but truly scaring a reader with fiction, instilling dread that almost comes off the page—that is not easy. If you've been drawn to *Shock Totem*, chances are you're looking to be creeped out, even in a world that feels like it's seen it all. And if you've read the work of Laird Barron, chances are you've already seen something shift in the mirror just as you turn away.

Barron is a genuine rarity in the world of horror fiction. His words are powerful and they do exactly what he asks of them. For more than a decade, he's asked them to scare you. To a truly admirable degree, they have in the most inventive ways. He has mastered cosmic horror, to the extent that I'll blaspheme and make the claim that in many ways he has surpassed the godfather Lovecraft himself. His first two collections, *The Imago Sequence* and *Occultation*, are simply brilliant and brimming with some of the most wonderful and effective stories I've ever read, regardless of literary reach or genre. The novel *The Croning* is one of the scariest books you'll ever read. They all prove his formidable talents.

But I've been intrigued by the facets of the author that go beyond that special gift. Explorations that have recently branched out and become more apparent in his work. Laird was kind enough to answer my burning questions, and he's provided good reason to be excited by where his work will take us in the future. He also succeeded in reassuring that part of me that always wants something creepy crawling on it.

~

MW: A lot of ink and pixels have gone toward discussing your Lovecraftian roots, so one can assume you were influenced heavily by H.P. Lovecraft, as well as T.E.D. Klein, Karl Edward Wagner, and the likes. But I've always felt your work goes deeper than that, rather than skimming the fat off the Lovecraftian universe. There's a good bit of hard-boiled noir in your work, as well as a gritty residue of Cormac McCarthy. The latter shares your essence of gorgeous words, bleak worlds, and the devastating use of geography and natural scenery. Could you give us a bit of insight as to your less-known

influences, perhaps outside the strictly horror genre?

LB: Michael, thanks. You have cited three major horror influences, and yes, McCarthy is another whom I greatly admire. Crime, noir, thrillers, westerns... these genres are ingrained in my style and influence the thematic elements of my core work. This is the stuff I devoured as a kid. I've mentioned Louis L'Amour and Zane Grey, Martin Cruz Smith and John LeCarre. But William Goldman's *Marathon Man* and *Control* figure in there, as does *Falling Angel* by Hjortsberg and *Smilla's Sense of Snow* by Høeg. During my teens and early twenties it was John D MacDonald, Donald Westlake, and Lawrence Block. *The Horse Latitudes* by Ferrigno is another favorite, and one that taught me how noir can swerve into horror and science fiction territory. These days I'm blown away by Gillian Flynn. She melds crime and psychological horror like nobody's business.

MW: And speaking of other genres, I find that your work has recently embraced more fully those shades of noir, hard-boiled protagonists, crime, etc. The horror is still there, but it doesn't seem quite as much the driving force; that is to say, creeping the reader out isn't, perhaps, your main priority these days. What are your thoughts on the horror genre today, and your place in it? What has drawn you away from both the pure, unspeakable terror of cosmic horror and scaring people in general? Do you think you'll ever leave it behind entirely?

LB: It's not appropriate for me to speculate upon my place in the field. I love the genre. Horror traditions inform my technique. The field is vital at the moment. The old masters such as King, Straub, and Barker continue to produce at a high level. Joe Hill, Sarah Langan, and Stephen Graham Jones, and a dozen others, are ready to take the torch. There is more quality dark literature coming out than I can reasonably keep up with. This might be a golden age of darkness.

I won't abandon the literature of horror or the fans I've gained in writing horror. I'm a morose, morbid guy and the macabre is my friend. There will be more horror novels, more collections.

Crime fiction attracts me, as do thrillers and noir. I also love the weird à la Aickman, Cisco, and Jackson. These elements have always been present in my stories. Arguably, many of my tales are three quarters crime/noir and the remainder is where the black fantastic seeps in. Regardless, there's a razor thin line separating the darkest noir and full-blown horror. It's only natural that I'd want to stretch myself as a writer, and to expand my audience. I love the Spenser series, and Smith's immortal Arkady Renko. One-offs such as McDonald's *The Damned*, and Flynn's *Gone Girl*, or McCarthy's *No Country for Old Men* energize me. I want to try my hand at that. I will.

MW: Pretty early in your career you seemed to be developing your own mythos in Washington State. The Black Ram Lodge, the dolmen and caves in "Mysterium Tremendum" and "The Men from Porlock," just to name a few, were revisited with different characters and even different historical periods. That dolmen even seeped into your novel, The Croning. I think fans appreciate that woven world-building. Do you still plan to set stories/novels in this mythos? Just your cosmic horror efforts? The "not so much horror" stuff?

LB: In the past I've said something to the effect that I'm veering away from the explicitly Lovecraftian mode. However, that doesn't mean I intend to abandon the genre. Some of this will be set in the same universe I've created over the years. If not the Children of Old Leech or terrors from the Black Guide, then something worse. There is always something worse.

MW: Creepy! Speaking of which, above I mentioned that one could gather that you've grown slightly less concerned with "creeping the reader out." When I tell people about your work, the one thing I invariably mention is that of every author I've ever read, you're the one who consistently, truly writes horror well at a visceral level. I'm talking skin-crawling, dread-inducing, disturbing, feel-something-in-the-dark-behind-me type of writing. While it would be exciting to read a novel by you that, hypothetically, doesn't have a shred of horror in it, I would miss that quality in your work. I'm talking not so much about the overall blanket of horror here (as I did above) but that specific quality of creepiness. We trust your literary talents to take you where you want to go, however. How do you feel about that brilliant creepiness and the possibility of lessening it as you explore other avenues? What creeps you out? And what about other genres, so to speak, draws you in the same way?

LB: Crime and suspense do it for me. Pulp westerns and noir do it for me. I enjoy mysteries and procedurals. Perhaps this new material of mine will serve as a contrast for current readers who've journeyed with me to the dark reaches of reality. Ultimately, the exploration of other genres allows me to expand my audience. That's not to say the new work will entirely lose touch with the disturbing or the unnerving. I'm working on some pieces concerning a protagonist named Jessica Mace. One of those, "LD50," flirts with the horror genre and if you check it out, you'll get a glimpse of my approach to injecting the macabre into crime/thriller narratives. Mace's ongoing saga sees her pitted against the ineffable and the monstrous. In its own way, her tale is as spooky as anything I've done.

What frightens me? Madness. Deep water. The immensity of space whirling above my head on an icy night. The inconstancy of friends and lovers.

MW: Another thing you do exceptionally well is folklore, incorporating it into your work, whether through the occult or through simply nailing authentic period pieces. How does the past factor into your worldview?

LB: Folklore, fairy tales, and mythology were staples in my house during childhood. I believe in the fundamentals. I believe in tradition. I believe in learning the rules in order to bend them, break them, remake them.

MW: If you had to choose one Barron short story as a favorite, which would it be and why?

LB: "Parallax" from my first collection. It's a science fiction story, a weird tale, which I wrote in response to the infamous Scott Peterson trial. My take on the mutability of reality, the paradox of time and existence. Took about nine months to complete that novelette and it consumed me, burned me up. It has never received much attention, but from a technical perspective it's probably the most technically ambitious piece I've attempted.

MW: What are some upcoming works that best represent your new direction (if "new direction" is what you consider it)?

LB: I think of this as an expansion, a process occurring in addition to what I've concentrated on in the past. My latest collection was written just prior to my current foray into crime and suspense territory: *The Beautiful Thing That Awaits Us All* is directly in the wheelhouse of my readership and it's a synthesis of the two earlier collections. A rogues' gallery of hard-bitten men and women beleaguered by forces alien and occult. Those stories reprise and crescendo what I've done these past twelve or so years. As for the really new stuff...first up is an Alaska-themed collection, working title of *Ardor*, that I'm putting the finishing touches on. Everything references the 49th state in some way. You'll encounter a bit of cosmic horror, crime, a couple of suspense/thrillers, a slasher. The whole thing is saturated with weirdness. It's a stark collection of stories. The prose is leaner and harder than what I've used in the past. There are a lot of dogs.

The other major project is a crime novel. I can't reveal much about it at the moment except that I'll be handing it in late this summer, or early fall. It's dark and violent. Men who are forces of nature collide. I'm hoping it's the beginning of a series.

MW: You mentioned your new collection, *The Beautiful Thing That Awaits Us All*. In closing can you give us a release date for that?

LB: The collection will be out in mid-August on Night Shade Books.

MW: Good, that's just around the corner. Laird, thank you for your time and your insight.

LB: It was my pleasure, Michael.

THE GATES OF EMILE PLIMPKIN: THE GRAVEDIGGER'S LEGACY

by S. Clayton Rhodes

"Whosoever is unclean by the dead shall be put outside the camp, that they defile not the camp in the midst of which the Lord dwells."

—Numbers 5:2

1

The first trip through the Gate of Remembrance, the name by which Emile Plimpkin eventually came to think of it, took him completely unawares. He had been tending vegetables in the modest garden he'd planted in early spring—something he did out of pure joy, rather than vocation, as his family had left him reasonably well off—when he noticed something amiss.

While Emile stood, leaning onto his walking stick, he noticed a brief shimmering around the edges of the white clapboard garden gate. It could have been a flash of lightning for all he knew, for the day was gray and the clouds swollen with the promise of rain, but he didn't think an approaching storm was the answer. This had been more like the sparkling a jewel will make when light hits its many facets than heat lightning.

Emile wiped perspiration from his brow, spanked garden sod from the knees of his trousers, then walked toward the gate. He unlatched it, then stepped through to investigate the cause of the inexplicable luminescence.

What he saw next caused his heart to fairly leap into his throat. Following a flash of white and the sensation of cold air blasting through his body, the dirt lane he expected to see beyond the gate, as well as the ancient and familiar sycamore with its broken boughs, was not there. Instead, a scene foreign to his eyes asserted itself...a landscape of stone markers. Monuments of every size and shape topped hillocks and filled dips of the rolling verge, and the scabrous claws of dead elms scrabbled at the myopic eye of a pallid sun. This did not seem to Emile to be the country in which he'd been born and bred but another entirely. It was a land comprised wholly of dead denizens who slept the eternal sleep beneath mile upon mile of bleached marble markers as far as one could see.

Emile's surprise was so profound he barely registered his own backward retreat until colliding with a granite obelisk. Only this interrupted his amazement, and then but briefly.

The gate leading to his familiar back plot no longer existed. The garden itself was not there. His meager cottage...gone.

To a man such as Emile Plimpkin—a studious man of academe who prided himself on his higher learning—it was impossible not to seek some immediate explanation for this phenomenon. More perplexing still was the question of how to return home from this abhorrent Necropolis in which he now stood.

But for the cawing of distant crows wheeling against sickly umber clouds, no sound fell upon Emile's ears. He decided he must be dreaming. Yes, that must be it. He was still abed, dreaming, or else going mad.

Determining there was no alternative but to see this (whatever "this" might be) through to the end, Emile resolved where there were dead, there must be living, and thusly set off in the direction of the setting sun. For a moment, he paused, wondering if in this nightmarish place the sun even set in the west, as well it ought.

2

Just before the sun reached the peaks of the haze-muted hills, Emile found his way to the edge of a village. It was not entirely unfamiliar, and that, too, was strange. In many ways it was reminiscent of his own Chapel Landing, with high steeples spearing low scudding clouds and shop fronts crowding the cobbled streets. But if it was Chapel Landing, it was a version from long ago, and the angles of the buildings were neither true nor straight. They canted in crooked lines, leaned in awkward planes. Again, it was a construct of dream matter, which both mystified and bedeviled Emile to no end, but it also served to fortify his theory that he must be sleeping, and this place would be but a memory come morning.

But then this did not have the feel of a dream.

He scanned the distorted avenues for some inhabitant to ask about his whereabouts, but there was not one soul to query. It was as if some epidemic had wiped every trace of humanity from the land. He called out, anxiously awaiting some response, but his own voice was the only one to return, echoing back in the most melancholy fashion from grimy brick alleyways. He tried shop doors, but all were stuck fast, almost as though they were mere set decorations of some stage play than functioning portals.

What was this place, and where were its people? Emile wondered should he retrace his steps to the vast cemetery and scrape back the earth from one of the graves, if he would find a corpse picked clean to the bone by worm and mite, or if that casket would prove as vacant as this city.

If this were truly a somnolent-state counterpart to Chapel Landing, it stood to reason the best course would be to locate his own counterpart home. So, Emile strode toward what should have been the Episcopal Church at the outskirts, but in this twisted adaptation of his own village, a crudely formed mill stood in the church's place. And yet, there his house lay beyond, altered less in detail than most other structures, though the brick proved in poor repair and the fencing remained unpainted.

The garden. The fence enclosing the garden.

The gate!

Emile couldn't round the corner quickly enough to try the entrance and test his theories, for it seemed to him this might be a means of return.

The latch was fixed.

He forced it. And went crashing headlong through, into and beyond a sheet of shimmering vapor, opalescent in color and cold as February frost to the touch.

On the far side, Emile collapsed to the ground, rolling over carrot shoots and breaking newly tied stakes and bean poles.

But to be away from that wretched dreamland!

Here the air was neither stale, nor still. Colors were rich, not bleached away. The sweet calls of song birds were myriad, and in such contrast to the loathsome cawing of crows winging above cold tombs, as in the other land. It was noonday, not approaching dusk.

And Emile hugged his arms about himself and thought, I am back!

3

As it turned out, Parson Harper had no erudite words of advice for Emile when he called upon him later that day. The murmurings of rain had broken into a full torrent now, and occasional hailstones pecked at the windows.

At first, Emile had been cagey in his approach, asking at the offset after the parson's daughters and their families, and then making light of such subjects as local politics and small talk of which congregation members had taken ill and might appreciate a word of prayer.

After a time, though, Parson Harper, who had known Emile but a short while, was able to deftly pierce his ramblings and discerned there was greater purpose behind the visit. With shrewd candor, he asked what Emile's true business was, as he drew upon his briar pipe and blew gray circlets at the parlor ceiling.

Emile hedged, the silence broken only by an erratic peel of thunder and the persistent tapping of rain upon the windowpanes. What if the parson thought him an imbecile, or at least going daft? There was a sanitarium in nearby Athena to keep those likely to do harm to themselves or others, and Parson Harper might well think such an arrangement appropriate for Emile once he heard his tale.

But Emile was no dullard. He first insisted on invoking the sanctity of his friend's office, asking for the parson's word as a clergyman he would not pass judgment or share his story with any other.

"I so swear." The parson humored Emile with a slight smile as he placed his hand upon his heart with exaggerated solemnity.

"Then I shall tell you," said Emile, "and afterward you may advise me as to whether the devil has overtaken my senses, and if so what I may do to protect myself in the event he might seek to do me future mischief."

Again the faint smile played at the corners of the parson's lips. "So melodramatic, Emile. But you've intrigued me, to say the least. Please, go on. I'm on the edge of my proverbial seat." So saying, the parson eased back into his chair and allowed his visitor to tell his tale.

4

At the end of the account, Parson Harper nodded while his eyes squinted to narrow slits in thought. But he confronted Emile with neither accusations of lunacy nor suggestions of seeking assistance from the local physician.

How long had Emile lived in the house, he inquired after a lengthy pause.

A score of months, as the parson well knew, Emile told him.

Again, the wizened pondering, nodding and blowing of briar pipe smoke at the plaster ceiling, yellowed from many similar sessions of tobacco indulgence.

Did the parson not think him mad then, Emile wondered.

The parson did not. In fact, truth be told, he had heard reports of many strange happenings which were rumored to have occurred in Chapel Landing, and the house in which Emile now lived had a most exceptional reputation unto itself. Like iron filings drawn to a magnet, stories collected around that particular residence to the extent that the parson was not surprised in the least to learn of yet another anomaly associated with it.

Emile's interest was piqued at once, but the parson would say no more of the matter. He instead insisted he did not wish to alarm Emile's sensibilities just yet.

"Best let sleeping dogs lie," he said. "Rest assured, if this should happen again, we may speak more on it."

Happen again? Emile shuddered at the thought. One such stroll through the waking nightmare he had been witness to was sufficient to last a lifetime, and he would no sooner attempt stepping through his garden gate again than he would through a portal to hell. Come to think on it, who was he to say they were not one and the same?

Yet, Emile did make his way through the gate again. The very next day, in fact.

5

It happened that Emile Plimpkin was very much intrigued with the history of Chapel Landing, it being the first settlement of the Northwest Territory and always an important stop of the trade routes. He liked nothing better than to pore over old texts replete with etchings of the founding fathers and the original steep-walled fort, constructed on the western side of the Muskingum to defend against heathen Indian attacks. Many were the hours he read upon the accounts of those first pioneers and their travels from Massachusetts, who eventually touched down at the promising settlement to seek new prosperity.

During such a study period, Emile found himself drowsing over a crumbling tome while sunlight warmed his back. It was not long before his chin rested against his breast, and his breathing slowed to sleep speed.

And then he dreamt.

He dreamt a dream of himself dreaming.

Outside of his own body, he watched himself rouse with a start, stretch, and leave the drawing room. From an umbrella stand, he plucked out his walking stick.

Emile believed he knew what was to come next, and thought, Wake up, you fool! Wake up before it is too late!

Sure enough, it was as he suspected. He watched, helpless, as his dreamself headed toward the rear of the house. Out to the garden. His dreamself moved in the direction of the previously discovered Gate of Remembrance—as he now thought of it—unlatched the hook, and pulled back the slide.

Upon seeing the rippling, mercurial glow of the plane beyond the garden gate, Emile once more shouted in thought. His dreamself might have paused if only for a moment, as if having heard the warning, but then he pushed on anyway and was in turn swallowed by the shimmering liquid floe. In that instant, the dreamself and the watching Emile melded into one being once more.

On the far side of the Gate, Emile was witness to a slightly different scene than during his first trip. The vast graveyard was present, certainly, but instead of approaching sundown, it was now full dark. A gibbous, waxen moon rode a midnight sky full of pinprick stars, and the lunar light shone onto the many chalk-white tombstones, causing them to appear almost to glow.

Once more, the gate vanished at his back as an evaporating vapor, closing off any possible return to his home place and leaving him in the company of stone slabs, graven cherubs, and lichen-crusted images of the Virgin with Child. Only in this instance, the holy image seemed somehow blasphemous.

Emile had thought the experience of his last passing through could not have been worse. He was mistaken.

The chill and darkness the night brought seized his brain and imparted to him an abhorrent despondency the likes of which had never before sensed. In some fashion, the emotion emanating from this place had the unique ability to seep into the very marrow of his bones. But what was all this? Why did Emile return to this particular spot, what significance did it hold, and what was it that the parson Harper knew but of which he would not allow himself to speak?

Emile could only take heart in the fact he was somewhat acquainted with these surroundings this time around. Even by night, he recognized a particular tree on a low ridge from before. If he should head that way, he would reach the Chapel Landing of dream, and thereby would be able to locate the way home as he had previously, provided things went as they did on his last hellish jaunt.

He was about to set off when he noticed some brief movement. Surely this must be a figment of his fraught imagination. Nothing lived here, save the crows, seen last visit but now curiously absent. And yet his gaze was drawn to one monument in particular; one which described the darksome image of a man in slouch hat silhouetted against the moonlight.

Emile took a step forward, if not to admire the monument then at least to marvel at the macabre mastery in its craftsmanship.

It was at that moment the figure turned its head. It was no statue but a live figure, which had taken notice of him.

Emile might have muttered a greeting had the words not stuck fast in his throat, so surprised was he.

A laugh, low at first but soon bubbling to a high pitch, met his ears. Apparently the man found humor in Emile's befuddlement, and in the next instant he kicked his feet out and hopped down from atop the tombstone. He drifted toward Emile, slipping eelishly between the stones so abundant on the moon-washed landscape.

He was short, roughly two-thirds the size of a typical man, and the clothes he wore were of olden style: short breeches, a waistcoat, and shoes with shining buckles.

That Emile could not make out the face for the slouch hat frustrated him a bit, for he preferred to see whom he addressed.

"Well met, friend," he said at last. "Have you become stranded in this place, as well? Perhaps you have passed through some gate of your own. What is your name, friend, and shall we attempt to solve this enigma together?"

For a prolonged moment only silence reigned, as though the figure were trying to decide what to make of this speech. The he cocked his head from side to side then looked Emile up and down, and he, too, spoke.

"Gots any gold, Doddy?"

6

The voice was guttural, base, and when the speaker took another step forward, some self-preserving instinct directed Emile to retreat, raising his senses to full alert. There was something about this man, who'd been lingering alone in this place of the dead, which did not sit well. And what of the gold of which he spoke? Was he some highwayman intent on waylaying unsuspecting passersby? And if that were the case, who did he expect, anyway, since this place seemed to hold no people. At least none living.

Perhaps this truly was some crossroads of other times and places, and this man knew something more than Emile. Be that as it may, Emile found he didn't care overly much for further enlightenment on the subject. Thinking it best to simply head for town, he nodded toward the figure and took his leave of him.

Only the graveyard squatter was not so easily discouraged. He followed Emile like a dark, noiseless shadow, weaving between tombstone and marker.

Emile hastened his pace.

The man matched his speed.

"Don't run, pretty Doddy. Leave me have some gold. Don't let's be stingy now. A mere coin or two will do." The dwarf quickened his steps until finally overcoming Emile, and with a cackle, he leapt up and over an aboveground vault, landing upon Emile's back.

Emile toppled over, collapsing to the dewy grass while his accoster's calloused fingers sought his throat. He did not delay, but twisted to one side, seeking to dislodge the smaller man. But what the dwarf wanted for in stature he made up in brute strength, and he hung on until the last. Then, once bucked, he hissed as might a feral cat. Now that his hat had been knocked aside in the scuffle, the stranger's face was clear in all its disturbing detail. Baggy, pocked flesh surrounded a squashed nose and baleful eyes. A cauliflower ear, as corrupted and gristly as a piece of porous corral, stuck out from his loathsome head. It could as easily have been the fleshy growth of a tree fungi for all its misshapen abhorrence.

"Do you not wish to play, pretty Doddy? 'Tis time to play. Yes, yes. Time to play...and pay." With a movement too sudden for the mortal eye to trace, the fellow brought out a knife, whose keen edge flashed silver in the moonlight. "Give over your purse and pay the toll, and your death shall be merciful," the man promised.

What? This fellow meant to kill him even though he could offer up some tithe? Did he think Emile some sort of lamb for the slaughter who would lie down and expose its neck with nary a fight? How foolish!

Emile bent low, his hands seeking and finding his walking stick, while his eyes never left his toadish visitor.

Instead of breaking and running at the sight of the larger weapon, though, the fellow's face split into a wide, gap-toothed grin. Mayhap his mind was as decayed as his face appeared. That or he was undaunted—perhaps even goaded— by the challenge.

He circled Emile, feigning with the knife as if to strike, most likely to test his opponent's reflexes. For his part, Emile brought up his staff to meet the blade, every time knocking it harmlessly to one side. But the blackguard grew more daring, more cunning, now passing the knife from hand to hand and back again so that Emile would have less chance of telling from which direction a jab might come. Then the man darted forward, at once gripping the staff and thrusting the knife toward Emile's midriff. If not for his quick turn to one side, Emile would have been run through, skewered as surely as meat upon a spit.

"I'll sup upon your spleen, Doddy, 'ere this night is done. Will cooks it in butter and serve some to your mother with a nice pint o' ale, I will." Spittle flew from the little man's mouth as he let loose more laughter—the sound of one whose brain is truly beleaguered with dark thoughts most foul.

Emile voiced his disagreement while jerking his walking stick free from the hoary paw which clasped it, then clouted the man upon the crown. While the other was dazed, he further scrabbled at a rock roughly the size of a pavestone and brought it crashing along the fellow's temple. It might have killed a normal man, but of course there was nothing typical about this chap.

Then Emile ran. Ran as one might with the very devil after him.

"Don't go now, Doooooddddddy..." the voice resonated between the tombstones. "Stay and play a bit longer. We've only just begun, we have..."

7

Time passed at a different rate in the dreamland—or so it seemed. It was not long before Emile entered Chapel Landing's counterpart and its moon-silvered avenues and cul-de-sacs. All the while, he had watched breathlessly over his shoulder, lest his adversary appear and take him unawares. It was with great relief he reached the garden fence and the return gate home.

8

The sun was just kissing the horizon when Emile made for the clergyman's home. No longer full night, and no sickly white rind of a moon. No more dreamland.

Within the parsonage, Parson Harper poured Emile a glass of excellent port to brace up his nerves while asking for an account of his most recent adventure.

Even sitting mere inches from the comforting warmth of hearth fire, Emile had to concentrate to keep his hands from shaking and spilling the wine he'd been given. When he had purged his mind of the experience through the telling of his second trip through the Gate of Remembrance, he admitted to an improved mood.

For the parson's part, his countenance took on a weighty expression. Then he asked the question which he said would decide it for him. "When did you come by that walking stick, Emile? I don't believe I've seen it 'ere last week."

Emile informed the clergyman he'd purchased it at an out of the way curio shop a week ago Monday, and, come to think of it, the shop keep struck him as more than passing strange. When Emile had asked after the price, the owner had replied in answer, "Pay what you think it's worth, kind sir," and refused to quote any amount. Curiouser still, unlike in most bartering situations, Emile's first offer was accepted.

Parson Harper rose, crossed to the halltree where the walking stick resided and took it up for closer examination. The oaken shaft had been polished to a high dark gloss, but the round ivory head was the point of interest. On one side was depicted an open, laughing visage, and on the other side a similar face frowned disparagingly.

The clergyman quickly returned the walking stick to the halltree then stared at his hands in such a fashion one might think he'd sullied them with cow dung. A moment later, he retrieved a cloth from the kitchen and scrubbed vigorously at his palms. Without hesitation, he then flung the rag upon the fire where it smoldered and smoked.

"I should have warned you at our last meeting," he said in an apologetic manner. "I truly should have, but there was no way of knowing for certain, and I feared speaking of such profane things aloud might actually serve to bring about more ill luck. It seems, though, ill luck, having found you in the first place, has no intention of being easily brushed aside."

"Parson, whatever are you saying?" Emile wondered with no little confusion.

9

It was the parson's turn to tell a tale, and he spun the dark yarn of a dwarf who once dwelt in Chapel Landing many years before. Sometimes known as Stumpy Joe and at other times called Digger. Parson Harper said Emile's description of his height and an ear so deformed it appeared as though a sort of fungus grew alongside his head confirmed his identity.

No one knew from whence the ugly toad of a man hailed originally; it was only known he showed up one day on the doorstep of a prominent townsman, asking for what food could be spared. The townsman took pity upon the deformed man and found work for him—a job no one else should want since the last person held office...that of gravedigger.

After a time, however, a shadow of suspicion fell over Stumpy Joe. He seemed to enjoy his work overly much, and children and animals both of which are always uncannily astute in their instincts—seemed to take particular care to steer clear of him.

"On the street," Parson Harper said, "they gave him a wide berth, though he had done nothing to that point to raise alarm. He was merely odd and solitary, and so was left to his own by and large. The town afforded him a little money for his service and in some years, he abandoned his shanty, building in its stead a humble home somewhat apart from the rest of the town.

"Your home, Emile," the parson said with especial emphasis. While he let this knew bit of information sink in, he continued his story.

It happened that something like a plague swept through Chapel Landing in seventeen-hundred-and-fifty-three. Whole families—husbands, wives and children alike—were found in their beds with their necks puffed up big as bullfrogs' and their skin darkening to the color of char. At first, panic ensued. The physicians at that time were stymied, as no one complained of prior illness; the families simply turned up dead.

By and by, the dark cloud of doubt trailing after Stumpy Joe became conviction. His carriage house was searched while he was out, and three sacks of a certain poison, commonly used against river rats, were discovered. How simple-minded Stumpy Joe must have taken the townsfolk for. Anything of value was missing from the homes of the victims—a too coincidental fact, if they'd truly fallen prey to a plague—and the furnishings of Stumpy Joe's home were certainly richer than one might expect him to afford on a gravedigger's salary. Too, the poison in his carriage house was the very same as had been reported missing from the town stores the previous month.

It took the townsfolk no great effort in deducing Stumpy Joe must have crept into the homes by night and put the poison into cooking flour or perhaps directly into well water. When the families partook of either contaminated food or water, they no doubt felt an overwhelming nausea and lethargy, which drove them to their beds rather than to seek out a physician; no time for that!

A mob of a dozen or so men tracked Stumpy Joe to the cellar of the funeral parlor. He had no formal training in preparing bodies, but it was his practice to cake the deceased in lime before planting them. It was said when the men found Stumpy, he had with him three bodies which had been awaiting burial—victims of the fabricated plague. Stumpy Joe himself had not a stitch of clothing on, and it was plainly apparent he'd been doing...unnatural things with the deceased. Not only had the bodies been interfered with carnally, but various organs were missing, never to be found afterward.

Terms exist—ghoul, murderer, necrophile, cannibal—but all fell short in defining those acts committed by Stumpy Joe. Such atrocities were an affront not only to God but to any who learned of them.

The men were outraged, as one might suppose. They at once took Stumpy Joe—who kicked and screamed and spewed all manner of profanities—and beat him with birch switches until he fairly died from loss of blood. Then they hung him from the neck until death finally did take him. Afterward, deeming him unworthy of burial in hallowed ground, they interred him in a deep hole on the far side of the Muskingum, laying him in, not turned toward heaven, but face down, toward hell. And there he resides still; as to the exact location where he rests, none can say.

10

Such an amazing story," Emile marveled, sipping at the heady port. "And so strange I should never have heard of it 'ere now."

"Do you really think so?" The pastor rose to add a fresh log atop the glowing embers. To be sure, a chill had seemed to grow within the room, despite the warming effects of the wine. "You are not from these parts, Emile, and there are stories aplenty not to be found between the covers of your history books. But this is not a tale of which any in Chapel Landing are proud to share. That it survives at all is because it has been passed down by word of mouth. Do not forget, many founders of this fair city originated from Ipswich...where some of the witch trials were held."

Emile recalled as much. He also understood superstition ran deep here, the beliefs being handed down from generation to generation.

The Pastor continued. "Given that, it is no small wonder, what with Stumpy

Joe's appearance and preoccupation with 'knowing' the dead, in the Biblical sense, that folk should come to suppose him a confederate of Satan. And believing thusly, it stands to reason why they should not want his name writ on any record. No account exists of him, save, as I have said, what has been passed down through verbal word. His is a whispered memory, surviving only as a warning to children to behave, lest Stumpy Joe take them in their sleep. Such are the ways of local legend."

Emile had indeed read of the short-lived "plague," but little reference was made to it. It was only mentioned the thing ended abruptly and nothing more.

"But the dreamland which I've chanced to enter..." he swirled the wine in his glass in thought. "Whatever can that be, and how is it possible to enter such a place which exists neither in time nor space?"

The clergyman pursed his lips. "You may trust, Emile, that I have given that no small consideration. Your account leads me to believe you have somehow become tied to Stumpy Joe, and you are entering the skewed reality of a madman. Rather his skewed perceptions when he had lived. Your residing in his very home, for whatever reason, has caused you to enter the inherent memories of an insane, albeit deceased, man. You are entering the salacious dreams of a ghost, if you will—slipping into the reality Stumpy Joe might have wished for if still he lived."

Emile shuddered at the thought, his hackles rising. Though quite fantastic, the parson's reasoning followed a logical path.

"But what of my walking stick?" he asked. "You've said nothing of it, though you seemed to take especial interest in it just after serving the port. What bearing does it have in all this?"

"Ah, yes." The clergyman nodded with a satisfied, if sardonic, smile. "There is that. The story goes the great oak from which Stumpy Joe was hanged was chopped down, the roots pulled up, and all was set aflame. All save...well, I'm sure you've guessed by now. Jonathon Shively—the same townsman who originally took Stumpy Joe in—crafted himself a walking stick from a bit of the timber. I suppose it was a memento of the event to prove, in a macabre sort of way, that justice had been served, and perhaps as a constant reminder to Shively to not allow kind intentions to cloud good judgment."

"And you believe my walking stick and this Shively's are one and the same?"

"The cane was described to me as having two faces turned in opposing directions. This would seem very specific to me, and the whereabouts of Jonathon Shively's original walking stick is unknown. It fell out of his possession at some point and was never seen again. Heed my advice, Emile, cast that staff away, and be quick about it! No doubt it is the catalyst which has brought upon you the waking dreams of dead Stumpy Joe."

Without further prodding, Emile stood and took up the walking stick. He brought it up as though to fling it upon the crackling fire, but the clergyman stayed his hand.

"No, Emile, not here! I'll not have even the smoke from that blasphemous thing sullying my chimney. Be off with you, but take care to destroy the infernal object as soon as you are able."

11

It took Emile no time at all to decide what was to be done with his walking stick. He walked two miles from the parson's home to the river. He raised his arm and cast it, as one might a javelin, into the choppy waters of the Muskingum. Better to have it travel on to the Atlantic than chance it somehow escaping destruction here.

Emile watched the dark shaft bob upon the water for a time, and when it dwindled in the distance—a mere dot too small to see without straining the eye—it felt as though a giant weight had been lifted from his heart. If Parson Harper was correct, and the memento of Stumpy Joe's destruction reposing in the home in which the fiend once dwelt truly were the catalysts behind the opening of the gate, this would surely sever any connection, and Emile would be troubled no further.

12

When Emile Plimpkin awoke the next morn, it was to the cooing of mourning doves beyond his window. Sunshine streamed through the bedroom panes, warming the room and letting him know the hour to rise had already passed.

It felt sinfully slothful, rising at such an hour.

Once dressed, Emile was about to break fast when his eyes befell a sight which made his blood surge. The walking stick he had cast into the river hours before leaned against his doorjamb as though it had never left his possession!

Emile now had to recheck his sanity. Did the staff have the power to return to him? Was it possible it had some will of its own? Had it perhaps overpowered his mind, hypnotizing him into only believing he had discarded it? Ridiculous though these thoughts might have once seemed, the events of the last two days caused Emile to not toss such ideas so quickly aside.

Once his initial anxiety subsided, anger gripped Emile. The stick was indeed a tool of Hades. How else to explain its reappearance? Before God, he would destroy the thing this time. He would reduce it to splinters, soak the shards in lamp oil, and set it all ablaze. Then, later, he'd salt all earth where any ashes touched.

But no sooner had Emile donned his boots and opened the door, but another shimmering portal formed in the instant he was stepping through. Too late, he realized, for he was already being sucked through to the far side. Too late to alter his step! A slight muffling of all sound—as though cotton batting had been tamped into his ears—was followed by the familiar caress of frost across his flesh.

13

In the dreamland, it was night again. It might have even been the same night Emile had left last time. The moon was in roughly the same position as before, looming large over the same vast plain of graves.

"Hello again, Doddy," came the voice Emile now recognized. "All ready for another row, I see."

The dim figure was silhouetted a short distance away.

Would that Emile had had the forethought to better arm himself for the occasion. Had he only the presence of mind to have kept either a pistol or flintlock on him, this matter would be settled presently. Phantom or no, he had felt Stumpy Joe's paws about his neck as surely as he would have had they been formed of real bone and blood, and if Stumpy Joe gave the impression of having substance, it in turn seemed likely he could suffer harm the same as any other man.

"I want no trouble from you, friend," Emile told him. "I tell you, I have no gold to give, but I also have no desire to quarrel. Allow me to pass unmolested and all shall be fine between us."

"You suggest I'll come to a bad end if I prevent you from leaving, Doddy? How would you hope to accomplish that? This is my world here. All the townsfolk of Chapel Landing sleep the long sleep, just as they should, and I have free reign to come and go where I please and when I please."

"Never mind that. Suffice to say, I'll make good on my threat if you dare to accost me."

"Brave words, pretty Doddy. Who are you, anyway, and how came you here? I have been wondering, for I've not seen a soul aside from yourself in a very long time."

Emile wished he were as fearless as the front he sought to put forth. In truth, his blood coursed faster at the mere thought of being here once again. In the end, though, he supposed it was more important to keep up a brave appearance. "I," he said, "am Emile Plimpkin. As for you, sir, I have no need to ask who you might be, for your reputation precedes you. You are Stumpy Joe—or Digger, if you prefer."

Stumpy Joe seemed taken aback by the mention of his name, no doubt not having heard it aloud for some decades. But how his expression changed Emile couldn't say, for his face was full in shadow.

Emile continued, "As to how I came to be here, it would seem I am the witless pawn of some greater power which wishes me here, be it God or devil I don't know as of yet, but I hope such information will be revealed to me soon."

Though Emile could not see Stumpy Joe's loathsome face, he would have sworn a smile broke within the shadows beneath that slouch hat. "And what of this place? I have learned it is of my own making. Do you not understand I can change things at will, alter the appearance of anything I wish to match my design.

You speak of God, Doddy, but do you not comprehend the only god here is me?"

"I admit," Emile replied, "this land is the product of your diseased mind. But you are a mere phantom, and I doubt you have much sway beyond these dreams. You, sir, have been dead these many years."

The figure shook in rage at this. His wide shoulders trembled and his hands fisted at his sides at the revelation. Perhaps here in this fantastic land of his own design he did not—or could not—recall his own torture by birch rod and subsequent execution. Perhaps, in death, all such memory had been wiped clean from the slate of him mind. Or, more likely still, such ill recollections had receded over time.

For whatever reason, Emile's statement had seemed to have rent open old wounds, and the dwarf let loose a straggled cry of pure anguish. "Noooooooo! You lie! 'Tis not true. I breathe as I stand, I eat when I hunger, drink when I am thirsty. I am no more dead than you. And less so than you will be anon."

With that, the squat man came hurtling toward Emile. In keeping with his boasts of being capable of altering appearances of the land around him, tombstones moved like liquid to one side to allow a straight path for Stumpy Joe. He ran at Emile with all the fury of a baited dog, ready to rake Emile's very eyes from their sockets.

Instinctively, Emile threw up a hand to ward off the attack, and what happened then amazed them both. Before Emile's outspread fingers came ripples of motion through the air, and when the ripples reached Stumpy Joe, they grew in proportion and sent him hurling backward as surely as if he'd met with solid matter.

Dazed, Stumpy Joe rose slowly to a sitting position.

"What be you, some demon sent to usher me on to hell at last?" He shook his addled head, while Emile stood, looking quizzically at his own fingers and wondering what new power was this he'd just discovered.

He assured the blackguard he was no more a demon than an angel—though in his own mind he again questioned his role in all this.

"If from neither heaven nor hell you were sent, you'll still see one or the other 'ere this night is done," Stumpy Joe vowed, yellowing teeth bared. Beneath his cloak, he unsheathed his wicked-looking dagger, which he threw with both unerring accuracy and uncanny speed.

Emile made to deflect the missile with the same gesture as before, but too late! The knife was already on its way. He succeeded only in keeping it from sinking into his skull by giving it something else to pierce. When next he glanced down, he saw the blade had been hurled with sufficient force as to cause six inches of the sharp steel to pierce his palm and extend from the back of his hand.

The pain was exquisite. It gripped Emile, radiating past his wrist and up his arm as blood coursed freely from the wound.

Knowing seconds were precious and there was no time to dwell on mere discomfort, he brought the back of his hand down firmly onto a nearby vault. This forced the knife nearly free; he wrested it the rest of the way, then let it fall to the ground.

Regaining his senses, Stumpy Joe rushed at him again.

Emile, gasping, took up his walking stick with his good hand and held it horizontally before him. Stumpy Joe skidded to a stop as if he'd hit a pane of glass.

Of course! The stick! Why had Emile not deduced it before?

"You see this rod of wood, you lumpy excuse for a man?" he said. "Heed me well, Stumpy Joe, for once it was part of the object of your destruction. I see in your eyes you know it to be true. Though you may not remember your death, you feel it. This was fashioned from the gallows tree from which you were hanged. And while your poison may linger in this dream place yet, this staff appears thirsty for your blood, for has it not led me to you on more than one occasion? I see its intent now. It is a cleansing thing, not evil, and if my guess is correct, it likely seeks to see you dead a second time..."

Stumpy Joe dropped to his knees and clamped his fists to his ears. "No! Do not torture me thus with such words. 'T'isn't true, I say again, and I'll not stand for the sort of lies you spin, trickster. I'll—"

"You'll what, little man? Carve your initials into my guts? You've tried that before, and a lot of good it did you. I still stand, having suffered only a scratch." A bit of a stretch that, since Emile's palm pulsed with pain so regularly someone as well could have been hammering railroad spikes into it.

The dwarf glared at him, fumed from where he'd been rocking on the ground in frustration. He ground his teeth and made to rise, but Emile's staff barred him from approach. Eyes darting around their surroundings, Stumpy Joe grunted, then gestured at the graves around Emile. One by one, each monument and obelisk edged nearer, hemming him in, crowding close like stalwart soldiers. Additional gesticulations made the ground grumble and quake.

Emile, in turn, swept the staff about him. The ground instantly grew still; the grave-markers exploded. Stone fragments rained down upon him, but far better that than to be crushed by the closing markers, and in a moment, only settling dust remained.

A screech escaped Stumpy Joe like the war cry of a savage. He strained, making claws at the sky, which caused thunder to roll overhead. Purple flashes of lightning forked down, veining the sky with violent light as the soil in front of Emile gave way to two skeletal arms of immense proportions. These giant appendages groped for him, their fingers the size of timbers twisting into the hems of his garments.

Emile knew if the enormous fists closed on him, it would mean his death. But somewhere along the way, fear had fallen away as Emile had grown more confident of his newfound abilities. He stepped deftly out of harm's way and made chopping motions with his injured hand. The cadaverous limbs collapsed, splintered, then melded back into the unwholesome mold from whence they had originated.

Emile further completed a scooping motion, and the ground directly behind Stumpy Joe caved in to form a depression in all ways resembling a freshly dug grave.

The dwarf's ravings at the meaning and insult behind this were scarcely audible above the cacophonous thunder. The boiling clouds flared from within, and wind howled as wildly as a banshee's call.

Stumpy Joe fisted his hand at his opponent, the gesture of which triggered the weeds beneath Emile to move. Tendrils of what resembled crab grass thrashed as live things, lengthening in proportions at first, then seeking to snare Emile.

Emile made two motions: a sweeping movement—which caused the bothersome stalks to wilt as from an immediate drought—followed by a thrusting of his walking stick. Ripples of energy pushed outward once more, hurling the dwarf back into the pit. And to be sure, Emile commanded the earth to swallow up the vile creature.

Stumpy Joe might have worked his way out, had Emile not sealed his fate with one final action. He dashed forward, fell upon the grave on hands and knees, and drove the stick deep into the clay. As Stumpy Joe's hand broke the soil, and as both he and Emile were gripping the wooden shaft, a bolt of lightning arced down from the skies, spurring sparks and blue worms of light to course through both men. No matter that the wood was dead and a poor conductor; the rules of nature held little sway in this land.

The jolt filled Emile, and white-hot brilliance crowded his vision until at last he collapsed.

14

Consciousness came to Emile in slow increments. As he sat up, he found his entire body felt as wracked as it might have had a team of horses galloped over him.

As for Stumpy Joe, Emile was certain whatever remnant of his existence had remained after his death was now gone for good. His hold here was fading. Monuments eroded, turning to grit, trees melted like dripping tar, and the wind quieted as the storm came to its end. When the moon appeared, if anything, it seemed brighter than before.

It took great effort to stand, but Emile forced himself to do so. Best to be on his way, wherever that might be.

And thinking on that more, he realized that by the time he reached the alter-existence Chapel Landing, it could very well be there no longer. As with everything else, it might vanish, with Stumpy Joe no longer here to hold the image fixed in his mind; and if that should happen, Emile would lose his egress from this place and would be forever be its prisoner.

Then it occurred to him that if he had been able to match Stumpy Joe's powers of manipulation of matter, he could very likely create his own damned gate. He experimented by describing a circle in the air with the head of his walking stick. As predicted, a brilliant round plane hung suspended in mid-air—a glowing, opaque oval of liquid.

Emile thrust his arm through, tentatively, then removed it and saw it had suffered no harm.

After a sweeping of his uninjured hand, the small trial portal disappeared and he created a larger one in its stead, adequate in size to accommodate his entire body. He concentrated on his destination, held his breath, and staggered through the doorway on weak legs.

15

As though from a vast distance, Emile heard his name called. The words grew louder; the gentle tapping along his jaw became urgent slapping.

Parson Harper's face loomed large above him, his brow furrowed in rapt concern.

The clergyman wasted no time in helping his friend to his bed, explaining he had worried when Emile came up missing.

Missing? Whatever could the parson mean?

"I mean exactly that, Emile. I've not seen you for better than a week, and knowing your excursions—for want of a better word—as I do, I naturally feared the worst...that you had met with some foul end in that alternate Chapel Landing of which you've toured of late."

Parson Harper went on to say he'd stopped by two or three times daily since he'd last seen Emile, in the vague hopes he might turn up and prove his fears unfounded. It was in this fashion he had found him, sprawled upon the parlor floor.

Emile nodded understanding. A week, though. How was it possible? He had ventured home by way of the gate immediately after grappling with Stumpy Joe. His struggle and subsequent return certainly couldn't have eclipsed a week, though.

He strained to say something to this effect, but his throat proved parched and raw, his lips cracking. Even swallowing took more exertion than he could muster.

The parson hushed him, insisting, "Rest now. Time enough for the telling later."

And with that, Emile's eyelids fell shut again.

16

Over the next several days, Emile awakened for brief periods. At one point, a physician looked him over, head to foot, and indicated he needed as much liquid as could be got down his throat. The widowed Mrs. Soames came by, as well, and between she and the parson, they fed Emile coarse bread soaked in broth, changed the dressings on his injured hand, and forced more brandy upon him than even a drunkard could want. If the desired effect was for him to sleep as much as possible, their hopes were realized in full.

On the fifth day, Emile was able to sit up for half an hour at a time unaided, and on the sixth he could feed himself, though it was necessary to use his left hand.

And on the seventh day, Parson Harper must have decided Emile had had enough of a restorative period, for he finally pressed for details. He drew up a ladder-back chair close to the bed, stroked his beard pensively, and said, "So, let's have your report. I'm sure you'll allow I've been patient long enough."

During Emile's testimony, the parson gasped at the appropriate places, grunted at others, but above all else held any remarks he might make until the end.

"That," he then said, clapping his knees, "is your most entertaining yarn by far. Without reservation. Stumpy Joe struck by lightning, no less." He stood and paced beside the bed, not restlessly, but as in great thought.

"Sly old dog," Emile inserted. "You've already arrived at more theories, haven't you?"

A smile turned up the parson's lips. "Am I so transparent as that? Wait, hold your tongue. I have no need of an answer on that. But yes, friend Emile, of course I have been pondering the matter."

"You do like a good puzzle, don't you? And what have you come up with?"

The parson reseated himself and drew the chair up ever closer, as a spinster might prior to sharing a choice bit of gossip. "Just this...the matter of your having lost a week of your life. It was only your first attempt at fabricating your own gateway. On the other occasions, it would seem that it was your walking stick which was in control, and you were only along for ride, as it were."

"Go on."

"I'd dare say you are more or less a fledgling in your abilities. It might be that you not only have gained the power to transcend space and enter alternate realities, but you are able to circumvent time as well. It could be that you simply misjudged the point of re-entry to our world. To that end, that you were able to come even close is a minor miracle."

Emile did not care for the laughter which followed the parson's assertions but supposed he was likely still out of sorts from his near-death ordeal and decided it best to let it pass.

"Anything else?" he inquired.

"Oh, to be sure." From the bedside table, the parson hefted a thick book, bound in cracking leather, with faded gold embossing. With apparent satisfaction, he opened it to a pre-marked place and laid it onto Emile's lap for his perusal. On the printed page were depicted two faces, the backs of their heads touching. One laughed while the other cried. The caption indicated this was a representation of the Roman and Greek god Janus.

"Janus? Why, those are the same faces which are on the head of my walking stick!" Emile asserted.

Again the clergyman allowed a parsimonious chuckle then continued. "Certainly, dear boy. And have you not heard of this god before?"

Emile admitted he had not, or if he had, he did not recall.

The faces of Janus, elaborated Parson Harper, were often used in theatrics to indicate comedy and tragedy, and though the use of the symbolic visages had traditionally been used through the ages, none could tell why.

"But," he went on to say, "heed this—and you may read for yourself if you like, and if you feel physically up to holding this great tome—Janus was also the patron god of gates and doorways. Gates and doorways, man! Finally ringing any bells for you?"

Emile sat stunned, trying to take all this in and finding it to be too much to absorb quickly. "But how can you, a man who advocates and upholds Christian ideals, propone such thoughts as ancient gods? Do you not believe this to be blasphemy?"

"Ah." The parson inhaled deeply. "There has been my biggest obstacle. Balancing my faith with my suspicions. I am coming 'round to believe, Emile, that there is a broader scope than what my narrow doctrines would have me think. What if the God we know is only one facet of a deity who has many facets and many guises? Would it be such a leap of logic to suppose all cultures might see him differently, all observations filtered through their own perceptions and frames of reference? Why, even the Bible tells us all mysteries shall be explained to us one day. If this is not a mystery, frankly, I don't know what is."

"So," said Emile, "what, in all this, was the thing which caused it to come about? My dwelling in Stumpy Joe's home, the stick bearing Janus's likeness? What?"

"I doubt it would be a great stretch to say it was a unique combination of all those things. The gods did like their sacrifices, and, as I've told you, Stumpy Joe was hanged from a tree from which that stick was fashioned. With Janus's two faces added—perhaps inadvertently—that only solidified the thing. And what was the likeness put upon but a cane...an instrument of travel! And, as if that weren't enough, according to this book on mythology, Janus received from the god Saturn, in return for the hospitality he had afforded him, the gift to see both future and past. For all purposes, when you returned home, Emile, you returned a week into your own future. Whether you wished it or not, you transported yourself at least seven days from whence you left!"

It was enough to make Emile's head spin. "I'm still not certain how this can be. Matter cannot vanish from existence, only to come into being again. Where was my body when my mind was in this dreamland?"

"This dreamland must have had substance on some plane of existence. Therefore, your body and your mind were resident elsewhere."

Again, this pushed Emile's sense of reason to its limits. But of course Parson Harper had had two weeks to dwell upon this, whereas Emile was only considering these theories for the first time.

"How can you be so certain?" he said.

The parson nodded, left a moment, then returned with an object, which he tossed atop the book still reposing on Emile's lap. "You had hold of that when I found you," he informed him.

It was Stumpy Joe's wide-brimmed slouch hat, and the fabric was as real as any other—not dream stuff to vanish when one regained his consciousness. "But I don't remember..."

"You don't remember retrieving this before leaving the dreamland? In your daze, that would be understandable. Perhaps in the last moment, you snatched it from his head to prove something to yourself. Maybe you were curious as to whether objects from the world of his construction could be brought back to this one. This serves as evidence the people of the real Chapel Landing were in jeopardy without their even knowing. Ah, I can see by the expression on your face you've no idea what I'm talking about. But what I held back from you was that the townsfolk here were being troubled by bothersome nightmares. All very hushed, and while you've lived here a while, to most you're still an outsider, so it's no wonder you've not heard any such whisperings.

"My point is that it is said if you die in your dreams, you die in reality. It would seem Stumpy Joe had returned to plague the dreams of these good people. Once he gained strength, who knows how far it might have gone had you not headed things off? You've done everyone a great service, though none will know of the exact nature of your heroics, save me. Speak of your adventures to anyone else and you'll surely be deemed insane.

"And if you should be tempted to share your exploits, against better judgment, I'd appreciate not mentioning my name or my meanderings of the Lord Our God and His possible correlation with Janus. Those of our congregation are not nearly so forward thinking, and I would like as not be driven from Chapel Landing in the blink of an eye."

Emile laughed politely and said he would keep this in mind if he should ever feel talkative.

Then the parson glanced down at the hat in Emile's hands. "A nice trophy, actually, and it appears just your size. It may prove advantageous against the weather when you go on your sojourns."

"I doubt I'll be going on any journeys," Emile said with a laugh and a shake of his head. "I've had enough adventuring to last a lifetime. Of that you can be sure. And now that Chapel Landing has been cleansed of the evil spirit of Stumpy Joe and the need for it is past, any special powers my old stick might have held have probably left."

Parson Harper was disinclined to agree. In fact, he added that now Emile had had a taste of adventure, it seemed to suit him. And again came the chortle at the audacity of his own statement, considering Emile's lengthy recuperation.

"But rest now, Emile," he said. "For you'll need your strength. I suspicion this is only the beginning for you, and it would be a pity to allow these latent talents of yours go to waste. You have not only passed through doorways to other places, but it seems to me you've opened a new one in yourself. I should not be at all surprised if your services should be called upon again. And at a time when you might least suspect."

S. Clayton Rhodes is the author of over fifteen in-print stories, as well as *The Wiz of the West*, a children's book based on a play by the Missoula Children's Theater, which is an alternate take on *The Wizard of Oz* theme. His stories have appeared in anthologies by **Apex Publications**, **Wildcat Books**, **Woodland Press**, **Ballybunnion Books**, *Six Gun Western*, *Necrotic Tissue*, and *Shock Totem*. His first stab at editing a horror anthology is *Legends of the Buckeye State*, which is slated for a Fall of 2013 release. At least two additional short stories will see print in 2013, and he is currently working on a novel and additional stories as of this publication.

In his spare time, he enjoys doing artwork and collecting film prop replicas, and his day job consists of work in the human services field. He lives with his daughter Rachael and three cats in Marietta, OH, which is the real life counterpart to Chapel Landing, a town in which many of his stories are set. You can find him at www.sclaytonrhodes.com, or look for his author page on Amazon.com.

Smoking, the Old Sergeant Remembers 30 Mins Past Ceasefire

by Dominik Parisien

He breathes in
a smoke and fire fox that crawls
down his throat walled like a shovel-dug tunnel:
    it sears the roots and rocks deep in his lungs,
    burns away the sour stink of unwashed bodies.

(Weary of waiting outside
their hole, he heard the fox beg
turn me lose, one last time
do it, do it, do it
and he did, said-screamed
Burn 'em out, burn 'em all, boys
    FIRE FIRE FIRE).

He breathes out
a smoke and fire fox that drags
out his throat twisted shapes burnt onyx black:
    it animates them, makes them crawl
    back in through his eyes.

Dominik Parisien is a Franco-Ontarian living in Montreal, Quebec. His poetry has appeared or is forthcoming in *Goblin Fruit, Stone Telling, Mythic Delirium, Ideomancer, Strange Horizons,* and *Tesseracts 17,* amongst others. He currently provides editorial support for **Cheeky Frawg Books** and is a former editorial assistant for *Weird Tales.*

Strange Goods and Other Oddities

Books, Movies, Music and More

Bigfoot Crank Stomp, by Erik Williams; Deadite Press, 2013; 152 pgs.

 I may not be the sharpest crayon in the box about some things. Hell, about a lot of things. But I was smart enough to know exactly what I was in for when I opened the package from Erik Williams and pulled out his latest novella, *Bigfoot Crank Stomp*. From its gloriously whacked out cover art of a tweaking Sasquatch rising ominously from a cabin basement to the Deadite Press logo on the back, I knew it was going to be quite a strange ride. I changed into my special pants for the occasion and began reading.

The twisted saga starts with Russell and Mickey hiding in the woods, surveying a cabin. The inhabitants have the TV so loud that the programming can be identified from yards away. They apparently like Animal Planet. Russell and Mickey are about to raid the cabin. Being the top-dog meth peddlers in the area they don't like the infringement of these cats. Weapons in hand they attack—a not-so-smart move that is about to prove deadly.

What they don't know, is that these new meth cookers have a Bigfoot. Chained in their basement and addicted to their product. They feed him bowlfuls of the stuff...just to keep him pacified. We are never really told how this gang of dope makers got him there. But they have him and they have him hooked.

What would prove a destructive catalyst, the Bigfoot had not yet been "fed" when the two set upon their rivals.

There's gunplay and bodies, chains break, arms are ripped off, and Bigfoot escapes. Then we literally tear off on the remainder of this 152-page journey into boondocks madness. Filled with a retired Marine sniper who hears voices, a plucky camper girl on a mission, a sheriff of questionable morality, and his deputies, and then we have our hero, the seven-foot-tall methed-out Bigfoot. This concoction is liberally seasoned with the kind of bloodshed, sodomy, and depravity that you cannot read straight-faced. It's ridiculous and so much fun.

Williams is a great writer. His short chapbook, *The Reverend's Powder*, is amazing. He didn't let down with *Progeny* or *Blood Spring*, either. A talent to watch for certain. Ease of prose and taut plotting are his strong points. As well as his chameleonic ability to go from "mainstream" horror to ridiculous bizarro nuttiness without missing a beat. If you want a quick read that will entertain, this is for you. If you consider yourself a puritanical person of high moral fiber and no sense of humor...

keep moving.

–John Boden

Isabel Jane, by Catherine Dale; Pendragon Chapbooks, 2011; 36 pgs.

Isabel Jane is a small, beautiful chapbook published by Pendragon Chapbooks, an imprint of Pendragon Press. A high quality, well-edited chapbook with a striking cover by Neil Williams, it contains two stories. The title story, "Isabel Jane," is a first-person tale of a teenage girl who is kidnapped and imprisoned in an older man's home. It's a timely story, especially after the horrors of the recent news story concerning three kidnapped women in Ohio who were held in their captor's basement for ten years.

"Isabel Jane" is beautifully told from the protagonist's point of view. There's an alluring, almost disconnected reality that we see here and there. Vital pieces of the story are carefully laced throughout and I found it to be an effective way to keep the reader slightly off-kilter. I loved this story. It was satisfying and darkly lovely. I found myself thinking of it after I had finished the chapbook.

The second story, "Teething," is an imaginative, surreal story about an antisocial man who finds a giant tooth growing from the ceiling of his bathroom. This tooth and his care for it—brushing it carefully, putting his arms around it, holding his ear to it in order to ensure silence from the chaos going on around him—juxtapose his non-relationship with the unfortunate woman who lives upstairs.

"Teething" is a study in loneliness and regret. Dale handles the story's heavy subject matter with a delicate hand. It filled me with quiet horror.

Isabel Jane was an enjoyable, if sobering, experience. It was difficult to read about two women in different but terrifying circumstances. There is a sense of foreboding and danger in this chapbook, but it's written in such a satisfying, dreamy way that it cannot be missed.

–Mercedes M. Yardley

Eerie, by Blake Crouch and Jordan Crouch; Self-Published, 2012; 286 pgs.

Haunted house stories will always have a special place in this reviewer's heart. One of the first I ever read was *Ghost Story*, by Peter Straub, and I was instantly hooked. They have been staples of my late-night summer reading for years, everything from *The Haunting of Hill House* to *The Shining* to *Hell House*.

When I first picked up *Eerie*, by the brothers Crouch, I was more than a little excited. I'd read Blake's Abandon, found it to be wonderfully creepy, and thought for sure this would be yet another addition to a subgenre of story I already loved.

The story of Eerie begins with a car accident in which young Grant and Paige Moreton lose their father. Oh, he survives the crash, but he's an invalid for the rest of his life (which in some ways is worse than death). The story then moves forward thirty-one years, and neither of these two children has handled life very well. Grant has grown up to become a detective with a drinking problem, while his sister, who has struggled with drugs and depression for years, is a prostitute. Their paths cross while Grant is investigating a string of missing persons, the paths of the men he's searching for leading directly to Paige, who, despite her status as a high-price prostitute, is in a sickly state.

The reason? A strange power is holding her in her house. And now it's holding Grant as well.

This is the main plotline for half the book: Grant and Paige trying to figure out what in the world has trapped them in the old brownstone while his partner, Sophie (a somewhat cliché yet still enjoyable character), searches for clues throughout greater Seattle. This part of the book is deliciously eerie, just like the title suggests. Strange things living under beds, sounds in the night, some demonic force making the siblings perform acts they would otherwise never even consider, a mood of impending dread...it is all there. I held on tight, prepared for a harrowing ride to either salvation or destruction.

Then the second part of the book kicked in, and it all fizzled.

What began as a genuine horror yarn became something much, much different. It began to sway into the realm of science fiction, which in and of itself isn't such a bad thing (I love a good genre mash-up), but in this case the direction the authors took just seemed to come out of left field. The tone of the work shifted, becoming self-serving and honestly a bit silly instead of working off the atmosphere of anxiety and terror that had been so carefully crafted over the first hundred or so pages. I couldn't believe it. What had begun with such promise simply stopped making sense and fell flat. I was quite disappointed with that.

Not that there are no redeeming qualities to *Eerie*. The complex relationship between Grant and Paige was expertly told, though the end does cheapen this aspect a bit. And as I said, the first part of the book is great. If only the authors had stayed on that path, or at least didn't decide to go for a shocking twist just to go for a shocking twist, then this could have been a special book.

As it is, it's only okay. Which makes me quite sad.

–Robert J. Duperre

After You, **by Prowler; Slaney Records, 2013; 9 tracks, 43 min.**

Do you like your heavy metal served bloody and dripping with horror?

If so, South Carolina's Prowler (named after the iconic film, *The Prowler*) might be of interest to you.

Shortly after forming in 2010, the band released a series of four EPs, *Part 1* through *Part 4*, each consisting of two tracks based on a horror-movie classic—*Night of the Living Dead, Halloween, The Lost Boys, Hellraiser*, etc. Earlier this year, my buddy Kieran O'Loughlin released *After You*, a full-length album that collected those four EPs and one additional track, through his label, Slaney Records.

(A great thing since the EPs were CDRs, which surely won't stand the test of time.)

Musically, Prowler's influences—Metallica, Slayer, Iron Maiden—are on full display. There is nothing here, stylistically, you haven't heard before. But standout cuts like "The Dead Rise Again," "Haddonfield," and the album's best track, "Knives for Fingers," make it easier to overlook such trivial things.

Despite my love of its subject matter and heavy metal in general, *After You* isn't perfect. Far from it. Lyrically the band keeps things rather bland and boring, offering up little creatively and instead just reciting movie plot points with seemingly little concern for melody and hook. For instance, this line from

"Book of the Dead," based on *The Evil Dead*: "record plays, incantations, trees attack Cheryl, hallucinations; Ash and her try and leave, the bridge rails bent back in the shape of a hand." Hardly lyrical genius.

The other major flaw is with the samples. Anyone interested in hearing perfect examples of songs seamlessly fused with horror film samples, look no farther than White Zombie and Rob Zombie. That's how you do it! On *After You* most of the samples are jarring, distracting, and out of place. And when they do work, they're not mixed well enough to do the songs any deserved justice. Such a shame.

All that said, *After You* is an enjoyable album, warts and all. It's easy to forget that this is a debut offering. One can hope that the band only gets better with future releases. And hopefully they find a better qualified producer/mixer, too.

If you're looking for a decent heavy metal album dripping with horror, give *After You* a listen.

–K. Allen Wood

Sole Survivor, **by Thom Eberhardt (writer and director); starring Caren Larkey; 1982; Rated R; 98 min.**

Long before the *Final Destination* franchise began giving new-millennial teens nightmares, this film had mined that theme. And is still creepier than anything those films ever attempted. Written and directed by unknown

Thom Englehardt, who would later in his career give us the cult classic *Night of the Comet*. With *Sole Survivor*, his first film, he creates a chilling and unsettling atmosphere, one that does not let up throughout its entirety.

The film opens with a horrific airplane crash. Denise, a young woman, is the only survivor. Soon after her  release from the hospital, she begins seeing things. Strange and ominous things. As horror film protocol dictates, she seeks advice from a psychic friend. Her friend gives her numerous warnings about cheating death, all of which go unheeded. Denise does her best to move on with her life and the fact that she somehow cheated the Grim Reaper.

She finds that she will not be successful in such an endeavor as Death and his minions seem willing to stop at nothing to claim what they were denied.

While the premise will seem played out, remember that this was made nearly twenty years prior to the *Final Destination* films. And wherein those films play, primarily on amped up CGI and how creatively people can be kill people, *Sole Survivor* harkens back to the old days of film, relying more on atmosphere and subtle creepiness over shock and gore. The subtle eerie feeling that permeates this film more than makes up for the hokey templates it seems to follow at times.

I discovered *Sole Survivor* when I was a teen and I was renting anything in the horror section of our local video store. I loved it, then forgot about it.

Fast forward twenty years and I overhear some kids at work raving the hip new movie they have just seen called *Final Destination*. I frowned and remarked that they had done that movie decades before.

When I went home and searched the Internet for some info on said film, I discovered that the fine folks at Code Red had given it a DVD release. I snagged it right away. It was every bit as disturbing as I recalled. Almost more so. Definitely shoulders above most of the shite that Hollywood tosses our way these days.

–John Boden

The Day and the Hour, by Ennis Drake; Omnium Gatherum, 2012; 41 pgs.

 This piece of long fiction isn't to be taken lightly. *The Day and the Hour* is a complex, carefully nuanced tale of tragedy, responsibility, decay, and desperate hope.

Ennis Drake introduces us to Jason Grae, a fatally flawed protagonist. After his death, Grae is shown some of the most tragic future scenes of destruction ever to occur on Earth. Dates. Times. Scenarios. What force is submitting him to these visions? What is the purpose? And what will Jason do with this unwanted responsibility?

He does what any of us would do.

Stands paralyzed. Tries to tune it out. Scrabbles after pills in order to escape. Breaks. And eventually decides that he will do what he can to make things as right as possible. A haunted man in a Florida Gators hoodie with a bat slung across his shoulder becomes a powerful symbol for all things right and simultaneously wrong with the world. People look at him with relief and horror, as either The Samaritan or the Angel of Death.

The complexity and intensity is characteristic of Ennis Drake's work. Drake, who was just nominated for the Shirley Jackson Award, writes with a raw, unflinching style that exposes emotions and realities that others shy away from. There's a surprising grace to his prose that softens the jagged edges of the dark subject matter.

This piece has a literary, experimental writing style. Occasionally the fourth wall appears to be broken and it can be distracting as a reader, especially if one is easily pulled out of the story. The time jumps and visions can also be distracting and it's possible to become lost. However, all of this chaos lends itself nicely to the overall schizophrenic feel of the story. If you want a breezy, linear read, then *The Day and the Hour* is not for you.

While Drake pulls no punches and seems to revel in the ugliness that he splays on the table, humanity still glimmers throughout. Whether or not Jason Grae's world goes down in flames, there will still be somebody struggling to stand until the very end.

–Mercedes M. Yardley

The Nine Deaths of Dr. Valentine, by John Llewellyn Probert; Spectral Press, 2012; 87 pgs.

Like everything else released from the UK-based Spectral Press, this book is a thing of beauty. It is a collectible hardcover, with rich, dark cover art, and a cool little built-in red ribbon bookmark—which we all know screams, "This is a classy thing, you hold here." And it's true.

The Nine Deaths of Dr. Valentine is a richly detailed and very warmly rendered love letter, to not only those gloriously overwrought horror films we grew up with but to the man who starred in so many of them, Vincent Price. Probert has crafted a novella that simultaneously lifts the plot from the cult-lauded Price film *The Abominable Dr. Phibes* and turns it on its ear.

We have a beleaguered inspector, trying to solve a series of bizarre murders. The murders are carried out in mimicry of famous death scenes from various films of Vincent Price. As the police come closer to solving the riddle-like crimes, we get some nifty surprises.

This was a very enjoyable read and a helluva lot of fun. I grew up worshipping at the altar of Vincent Price. Stood by him from *The Last Man on Earth* and his later appearance on *The Muppet Show*, right up to his final screen credit as the sad and lonely inventor in Tim Burton's classic, *Edward Scissorhands*. I am quite certain, that were Price alive today, he would adore this book. It is sincere in its jovial flattery. It is honest in its giddy adoration. This is an honest, fun, and very well-written novella. Track it down.

–John Boden

MediEvil, developed by SCE Cambridge Studio; published by Sony Computer Entertainment, 1998; Playstation

Yeah, okay, this takes me back. Takes me waaaaay back to college, sitting on the floor eating Wheat Thins with my then-boyfriend, and marveling at the super amazing Playstation graphics. Which were so much cooler than SNES graphics, right? I mean, there were little movies and stuff!

Fast forward to today. How would one of my favorite games hold up? The Playstation 2, unlike the majority of the PS3s, are backwards compatible, which means that they still play the original Playstation games. Which...I'm sure most of you know. This is in case your mother is reading this. Or mine. Hi, Mom!

The first thing I had forgotten is that the PS2 still had chords attaching the controllers to the console. It's been a while since I grabbed a little banana chair and scooted closer to the TV so the cord would be long enough, but it wasn't bad. Except that my little ones kept running into, falling, and tripping over the cord, which unplugged the controller during delicate on-screen situations. That...wasn't so much of a concern during college.

The game itself held up beautifully. Sir Daniel Fortesque, the hero of Gallowmere, was famous for slaying the evil wizard Zarok during a big battle. In all actuality, Sir Dan was the first casualty on the field, shot through the eye with an arrow and killed before the battle had even really started. One hundred years after the battle, Zarok is back. He raises up an army of undead, including our skeletal Sir Dan, who is forced to defeat Zarok for real. If he can.

The game is charming. Dark in a humorous, Tim Burtonesque vein. There are plenty of laughs sprinkled throughout. Our poor protagonist is constantly the butt of scathing commentary, looked down on by gods and sarcastic gargoyles alike. The dialogue is witty, reminding me slightly of Tim Schafer games. Much is made out of Dan's missing jaw and eye, and he occasionally mumbles back unintelligible retorts.

Gothic scenery and Danny Elfman-like music add to the dark whimsy. When this was created, 3D games were new. There are a few ticks and bugs that make *MediEvil* a little difficult, especially when it comes to gameplay. A tiny controller nudge here or there sends Dan flying off a cliff or into lava. I was occasionally irritated by how carefully I needed to line up my jumps (across rocks, onto floating caskets, etc.), but it certainly didn't dampen my enthusiasm for overall gameplay.

There are several secret areas to discover, and plenty of incentive to replay game levels. Bosses easily reveal their attack patterns, and are fun but not too challenging. There are several amusing details, too, like sticky-fingered imps that steal your swords and sell them to greedy gargoyles (I literally ripped Dan's arm off of his body and used it as a melee weapon until I bought my sword back) and chilling, singing little possessed girls.

As I mentioned above, *MediEvil* held up, and beautifully. It's 15 years old, of course, and that needs to be taken into consideration. But it's also funny, enjoyable, and as satisfying now as it was back then.

–Mercedes M. Yardley

INTERESTED IN HAVING YOUR MATERIAL
REVIEWED IN AN UPCOMING ISSUE OF
SHOCK TOTEM
OR ON OUR WEBSITE?

PLEASE E-MAIL US AT
REVIEWS@SHOCKTOTEM.COM

The Horror That Et My Pap—and Other Swamp Stuff

by William F. Nolan

This here account is bein tole by me in the First Person. That's when nobody else tells it. That's me, the First Person. I could have tole it in the Second or Third Person but these other two ain't intimate enough. I learnt all about these three Persons in school, so if I have to use em I got em in my head, all proper fer the usin.

Guess I oughta start with how a gator we call "Big Boy" et my Pap. He's a real horror, Big Boy is. Got long toothy jaws fit fer chompin. Pap, he liked to likker up on weekends an what I'm telling happened on a weekend. Pap was skunk drunk and couldn't walk steady. Fell flat ass inta the swamp offa the ole rotty wood dock we fish from, which is when Big Boy slid up and et him. You could hear Pap's bones snappen as Big Boy chomped him up real proper. A rare sight ta see.

Now Pap's bein et was no loss at me an that's a fact. Pap was mean as a sow on Sunday. He'd whup me on my rosy butt with that leather belt that held up his britches. Ma, afore she passed on, usta try an calm Pap down, but it never helped none. He'd back hand her alongside the head. Smash her silly, then go right ahead with the beatin of me. Hurt like blue blazes.

Pap was one mean son of a bitch, that's fer sure.

Then there was my first cousin Elford who drowned in the Sabine River. Thin as a starved goat with bug eyes and no hair on top. Bald as a bean. Anyhow, Elford usta fancy a late afternoon swim in the Sabine. On this particular day he got snake-bit an then a undercurrent grabbed him. My goddies, but he was a pure mess when we finally drug outa the river—all swole up like a pufferfish with his eyes rolled up white as eggs. When we tole his mud-ugly common law wife, Letty May, how we found him she threw a fit. Tore her hair like them Injun wommen back on the plains. Hollered like a stuck hog.

As I stated previous, cousin Elford was a real mess when we drug him ashore. Looked like God's wrath fer sure. He'd been there in the river fer quite a spell an he was all blue an smelt something fierce. Take my word, you don't never want to smell like what cousin Elford smelt, I guarantee. No sir, never.

Well, I got me plenty more to tellya bout life here in swamp country, but I'm tuckered out, so I'll save it fer another time. So here I am, sign'n off.

In the First Person.

William F. Nolan writes mostly in the science fiction, fantasy, and horror genres.

Though best known for coauthoring the acclaimed dystopian science fiction novel *Logan's Run* with George Clayton Johnson, Nolan is the author of more than 2,000 pieces (fiction, nonfiction, articles, and books), and has edited twenty-six anthologies in his fifty-plus year career.

Of his numerous awards, there are a few of which he is most proud: being voted a *Living Legend in Dark Fantasy* by the International Horror Guild in 2002; twice winning the *Edgar Allan Poe* Award from the Mystery Writers of America; being awarded the honorary title of *Author Emeritus* by the Science Fiction and Fantasy Writers of America in 2006; and receiving the *Lifetime Achievement Award* from the Horror Writers Association in 2010. Nolan resides in Vancouver, WA.

Shall I Whisper to You of Moonlight, of Sorrow, of Pieces of Us?

by Damien Angelica Walters

Inside each grief is a lonely ghost of silence, and inside each silence are the words we didn't say.

~

I find the first photograph face down on the mat outside the front door. In a rush to get to the office, I tuck it in the pocket of my trousers, thinking it a note from a neighbor. An invitation to dinner maybe.

I pull my car onto the highway, into a mess of brake lights and angry horns, and shake my head. Morning traffic is always the same. Not sure how anyone could expect otherwise.

When I reach for my cigarettes, I pull out the photo instead—you, with a lock of your hair curling over one cheek, the trace of a smile on your lips, and your eyes twin pools of dark, a touch of whimsy hidden in their depths. Beautiful. Perfect. A spray of roses peeks over your shoulder, the blooms a pale shade of ivory. Far in the distance, a faint strain of music, your favorite song, echoes away.

The surface of the photo is slick beneath my fingertips, and when I lift it to my nose I catch a hint of perfume. Sweet and delicate, but with an undertone of some exotic spice. I will never forget that smell.

I close my eyes tight against the tears. Yes, tears, even after all this time. I knew you'd find me. I've always known.

~

Please let me go. Please.
Never.

~

In the middle of the night I wake to the smell of flowers. I move from room to room with a dry mouth and a heart racing madness, turn on all the lights, and check the windows and doors. Locked or unlocked, it doesn't matter. If you want to come back, they won't stop you. Nothing will. The photographs are proof of that. Still, the locks are a routine that makes me feel as if I'm doing something other than waiting.

I peer through the glass to the back yard where moonlight is dancing across the grass. The tree branches sway gently, like a couple lost in the rhythm of a dance. I whisper your name, my voice breaking. Only house noise answers. I rake my fingers through my hair. I don't know if I can go through this again, but I also know I have no choice.

I never did.

~

The next photo appears face up on the coffee table in the living room. Same smile, but with your hair pulled back in a ponytail. A thin silver chain circles your neck; the fingertips of your right hand are barely touching the small medallion hanging below the hollow at the base of your throat. A trace of dark shadows the skin beneath your eyes.

Baby, those shadows say.

Yes, I still remember the sound of your voice.

I fumble a cigarette free from the pack; it takes three tries before I can hold my lighter still enough to guide the flame where it needs to go.

When my job transferred me from one coast to another, I thought the distance would be too great for you. Even when I still lived in the old house, it had been over a year since you left the last photo. I'd thought you were gone.

I know it won't be any different this time, no matter how much I want otherwise. This hope is a strange thing, a wish wrapped in barbed wire. Or maybe delusion.

~

The smell of flowers again in the middle of the night. I stay in bed, the sheet fisted in my hands. Heart full of chaos; head full of images.

~

My coworker catches me at the end of the day when I'm slipping into my coat. "Hey, a bunch of us are going to happy hour. Want to come?"

"No, maybe next time."

He raises his eyebrows and shakes his head. "That's what you said the last time."

"Sorry. I already have plans."

"You said that, too."

I shrug one shoulder and step away before he can say anything else.

~

I sit with the television on mute, listening to the silence. A book sits unread on the sofa beside me; a glass of iced tea, long gone warm, rests on the table. Condensation beads around the base of the glass like tears.

The minutes tick by. The hours pass. I listen to nothing. I wait.

~

Another photograph. On the bottom step of the staircase this time. You, captured on a blue and white striped blanket, shielding your eyes from the sun. Even in the frozen bright, the shadows under your eyes are visible and your skin is too pale. Next to you on the blanket is a crumpled napkin, a plastic cup on its side, a bit of cellophane wrap holding a rainbow's arc on its surface, a few grains of sand. I hear the rush of a wave as it touches the shore, then another as it recedes. The salt tang of the ocean hovers in the air, but only for an instant.

~

I smell flowers in the night. Maybe it's my imagination, but the scent is growing stronger. A promise or recrimination?

~

The landing at the top of the stairs. The next photo. Your face half in shadow, half in light. The almost-smile is still there in spite of the pallor of your skin, the hollows beneath your cheekbones, the scarf wrapped round your head. I hear the last breath of a laugh. Smell honeysuckle drifting on a cool breeze.

Always the same photographs in the same order. I don't know how, but the how doesn't matter. And I already know the why.

(Please let me go.

Never.)

It will be the last photo, just like the last time. I know it will, but I check the locks anyway. Everything is as it should be. It's too cold to leave the windows open or I would.

~

A throat clears. I look up to see my boss standing in my office, a small frown on his face. "Are you okay?"

"Yes," I say. "Why?"

"You look a little tired, that's all."

"Just a bout of insomnia," I say. The lie slips easily from my tongue.

"You have my sympathies. My wife's had that for years. Try a glass of wine before bed. That helps her."

"Will do."

He lingers for a few moments longer, and for one quick instant I think of telling him everything. I tried that once with your sister; she told me I should talk to a doctor, and then she stopped answering my calls.

~

I unlock the windows, as always, but my hand remains on the lever. I am so tired of waiting. I'm wearing shadows under my eyes now and I have a knot in my chest that won't go away. Maybe I could learn to forget about you. To move on. Throw away the photographs, let time fade the memories. Lock the doors and the windows instead of unlocking them. Go out with my coworkers. And maybe you'll stop.

I flip the lock, sigh, and turn it back. No, I want you to come back. It's what I've always wanted. Maybe that small sliver of doubt is the reason you haven't yet.

~

And then I find a photo in the hallway just outside the bedroom door. I sit with my back against the wall. I've never seen this photo before. You've never made it this close.

The smile is no longer a smile, but a grimace. The shadows beneath your eyes are now bruises of dark. I taste the bright sting of antiseptic. Hear the ticking of a clock winding down and down and down.

"Please, baby, please," I whisper, my voice hollow.

I take that tiny trace of doubt and shove it away. Hold the photo to my chest. This time will be different. I know it will.

~

I toss and turn for hours, listening to the quiet. The distance between the hallway and the bed seems so small, yet miles, worlds, apart as well.

Please, baby. Please.

The last words you said to me.

~

The next door neighbor is outside watering her plants when I get home. She waves. Smiles. I return the gesture, but not the expression. When she starts to head in my direction, I hightail it into the house. Rude, I know, but she caught me when I first moved here and kept me outside for an hour, her voice flitting from topic to topic like a bee out on a mission for nectar. She doesn't pick up on any of the signs that I want to be left alone, or maybe she does and just chooses to ignore them. The way she ignores the ring on my finger.

~

Another photo, left on the foot of our bed. It shows only clasped hands. Matching silver bands. Fingers entwined. One hand is hale and hearty; the other frail, the veins standing out like mounds in a field of fresh graves. I feel the paper skin beneath my palm. I hear a whisper of words, promising lies, promising everything. I taste a kiss laced with despair and loss.

I can't stop the tears. I can't stop my hands from shaking. But I run to the florist and buy three dozen red roses, long-stemmed with thorns, the way you like them. On the way back, I brave the mall and buy a fresh bottle of your favorite perfume.

~

But one day becomes two. One week turns three. No trace of flowers in the air. No new photos. I'm still alone with empty arms and a knot in my chest. I smoke cigarette after cigarette. Pace footprint divots in the carpet. Choke back tears as the hope leaks out, a little more with each passing day.

My boss was wrong about the wine. It doesn't help at all. Nothing does.

~

After two months, I slide the photographs into an envelope, tuck the flap over as best as I can, and pull a battered shoe box out from under the bed. Nine sets of photos. Ten envelopes, the last one sealed. The paper clearly reveals two small circular shapes. The saint on the medallion never offered assistance; the ring is only a circle of empty without your skin to bind it.

When I close my eyes, I recall every plane and curve of your face, before illness turned you pale and hollow; but I wonder...if not for the photographs, would I? Would time have turned my heart to scar instead of open wound?

I shove the box back under the bed, my mouth downturned. I should've known better. You've tried nine times in five years. All the want in the world can't bring you back.

~

The next time my coworkers ask me to go to happy hour, I say yes. I say yes the second and third time, too. By the fifth time, I don't have to force a laugh at a joke or fake a smile when someone catches my eye. I feel a loosening in my chest. An ease in my breath.

I take the box of photographs and put them on the top shelf of my closet. I make sure all the doors and windows are locked before I go to bed. And, finally, I take off the silver ring. My eyes burn with tears, but I blink them away before they fall.

~

"Please let me go," you whispered through cracked lips. "Please."

"Never," I said, arranging the scratchy hospital blanket around your shoulders.

Your bare scalp was hidden under a yellow scarf, but nothing could hide the matchstick legs, the grey tinge of your skin, or the pain in your eyes that morphine couldn't touch. No amount of perfume could mask the shroud of illness and breaking hearts.

I held your hand and told you for the thousandth time about that night, our first date, after I dropped you off. How I turned and saw you standing with your hair full of moonlight and your lips full of smile. How I knew I would spend the rest of my forever with you.

"Please, baby, please."

And then only silence. I sat with your hand in mine until your skin began to cool. I didn't cry until a nurse led me out of the room.

~

I wake on a cool morning in early autumn to find the photograph on the mat outside the front door. The lock of hair, the little smile, the pale roses. I stand with my hands in my pockets for a long time, but eventually I carry the photo back into the house.

I'll leave the windows open every night, weather be damned. I'll put flowers out every day. Because you were so close the last time. So very close. That has to mean something.

I slip the ring back on my finger. It was a mistake to take it off in the first place. I won't make it again.

Please, baby, find your way back home to me. I'll wait for you no matter how long it takes. I promise I will. If you make it all the way this time, I'll say the goodbye I should've said in the hospital.

Maybe then I'll be able to let you go.

Writing as **Damien Walters Grintalis**, Damien's short stories have appeared in magazines such as *Beneath Ceaseless Skies, Strange Horizons, Interzone, Fireside, Lightspeed,* and *Daily Science Fiction,* and her debut novel, *Ink,* was released in December 2012 by **Samhain Horror**. Her work is forthcoming in *Shimmer,* the anthologies *Glitter & Mayhem* and *What Fates Impose,* and a collection of her short fiction will be released in spring 2014 from **Apex Publications**. She's also an Associate Editor of the Hugo Award-winning magazine, *Electric Velocipede,* and a staff writer with *BooklifeNow,* the online companion to Jeff VanderMeer's *Booklife: Strategies and Survival Tips for the 21st Century Writer.*

You can find her online at www.damienangelicawalters.com or follow her on Twitter @dwgrintalis.

BLOODSTAINS & BLUE SUEDE SHOES

by John Boden and Simon Marshall-Jones

PART IV: THE SIXTIES

I (Simon) remember watching a documentary on the late 60s hippie movement, wherein a "spokesperson" for the movement announced to the crowd gathered at some festival that he had returned from a fact-finding mission abroad, ending with the words, "It's happening!" The spokesperson's name remains unremembered, but that phrase epitomizes the optimism that carried the whole love-generation along. It was a hope that all wished would materialize—sadly, it was not to be.

I'VE SEEN THOSE SHADOWS...

At the beginning of the seventies the psychedelic tides had turned, leaving behind a petrified forest of those cherished ideals the hippies had espoused so fulsomely. The peace and love that had been in the air was now slowly being suffocated, choking on its own poisoned ethos, and was destined to fall to the ground like diseased cherubs. The love-in that had been a major part of the 60s was in the final throes of a brutal death by the end of that decade.

If there was a definite moment in which the final nail had been driven in the coffin of the 60s it would in all likelihood be the free concert at Altamont Speedway in 1969.

Of all the participating bands, Santana, The Flying Burrito Brothers and The Grateful Dead (the Dead actually declined to play their set, due to increasing violence and bad vibes at the venue), it would be The Rolling Stones who would be most remembered. During their set, which closed the festival, a rattled Mick Jagger repeatedly pleaded with the crowd to calm down. The set was stopped a few times to accommodate the pleas. During "Under My Thumb," a young black man named Meredith Hunter tried to access the stage with a throng of other fans. He was violently repelled by two members of the Hell's Angels motorcycle club, who were serving as security for the gig. Moments later Hunter returned to the front of the stage, drew a .22 caliber revolver from his lime-green suit jacket, and pointed it toward the stage. It is unclear whether or not he fired the weapon, though video of the incident suggests it is possible. What is clear, however, is that after brandishing the gun Hunter was stabbed to death by a member of the Hell's Angels.

The incident was yet another hemorrhage to the already weakening ideals of peace and love, a crimson smear on the doorway into the next decade.

Inevitably, there was bound to be a backlash against the failed hippie ideals of "peace and love." In addition, around about this time the US was embroiled in an attritional war in Vietnam with the Viet Cong, the communist organization opposed to both America and the South Koreans. The war dragged on and on, polarizing opinion in the US and causing discontent, leading to riots at home and mass protests around the world. There were also continuing racial tensions to add fuel to the mix of discontent—altogether a heady cocktail, which sought an outlet. And, as is often the case, out of all this turmoil emerged new creative forces and modes of expression in popular culture—especially in the field of music.

Alice Cooper (born Vincent Damon Furnier) is perhaps the most famous "shock rock" artists of all. Prior to his fame as one of the prime progenitors of the close association between rock music, the macabre and the grisly, he'd been a member of various bands throughout the 60s. His debut album, *Pretties for You*, was released in 1969, but it caused nary a blip on the musical radar. At this time, the name Alice Cooper referred not to the singer's identity, but was instead the name of the whole band. It wasn't until the release of the *Easy Action* album in 1970, however, that the band started to slowly metamorphose into the notorious entity people know them as today. Songs like the bombastic "Return of the Spiders" and "Refrigerator Heaven" were merely tantalizing glimpses of what was to come later as the decade sprawled out. They developed an outrageous stage show that would never be trumped for sheer theater, accompanied by an arsenal of material bridging such family friendly subject matter as necrophilia, dental misdeeds, giant spiders, murder, and all manner of mayhem, and all created by one of the tightest musical combos ever to grace a stage.

...AS THEY'RE MOVING IN MY SLEEP

While the heavies of the late 60s like Led Zeppelin and Black Sabbath were still slackening jaws with their primal rock styles (and they would continue to do so, becoming major influences on later bands), new and interesting things were brewing elsewhere.

Just then the UK was priming to deliver one of their best: Genesis. Starting out as a straight pop act they quickly evolved into an intense progressive rock band known for their elaborate songs as well as a stage show featuring costumes, pyrotechnics, and detailed sets. Fronted by Peter Gabriel, an innovative musician in his own right, the band became an audacious behemoth to be reckoned with. It takes some stones to deliver a twenty-three minute opus about one's inevitable demise ("Supper's Ready").

In 1974 the band would release their benchmark album *The Lamb Lies Down on Broadway*, which would also be their last to feature Gabriel as their dynamic frontman. *Lamb* seemingly concerns the adventures of a boy forced to journey through the underground and save his brother, in which he faces many surreal and frightening creatures and obstacles. But if one digs deeper there is an allegorical thread detailing the loss of self and the subsequent rediscovery of one's identity. As groundbreaking as they were in their early years, the band would sadly go through many personnel and stylistic changes before calling it a day after toiling through the 80s and early 90s as an anemic pop machine. It is worthy to note that, during the same period, ex-frontman Peter Gabriel released consistently challenging albums, full of the sinister edginess and often dark themes that made Genesis such a great musical force initially.

At roughly the same time, Malcolm John Rebennack, Jr. (more famously known as Dr. John) was gaining notoriety playing his wild amalgamation of rhythm and blues infused with voodoo chants and tribal instrumentation. Jaunty jazz and blues with a little funkification was, and still is, his signature sound. However, it wasn't always about mass consumer appeal and cranking out the hits. Were that the case we would never have seen the likes of acts such as Louisiana's own anonymous darlings, The Residents, who, throughout their existence, have ostensibly attempted to operate under anonymity, instead preferring to have all attention focused purely on their output rather than the identities of its members. Much outside speculation has focused on this aspect of the group, rumored possible members have included folks from magician Penn Gillette and Primus frontman, Les Claypool to one bizarre theory that they were, in fact, members of the Banana Splits. In public, the group is silent and costumed, often wearing eyeball helmets, top hats and tuxedos—a long-lasting costume now recognized as its signature iconography.

Musically, their ultra-bizarre stylings left most listeners flabbergasted. Utilizing samples and wild electronic sounds in addition to more traditional instrumentation, they've inevitably produced something which is entirely unique and instantly unforgettable. They're well-known for crafting entire albums of off-kilter cover versions of classics and current pop fodder, as well as penning original and surreal songs such as "Smelly Tongues," "Monkey & Bunny," "Semolina," and too many others to list. But just to prove that quirkiness is next to godliness, The Residents are still going strong and we still don't know who the fuck they are—in all likelihood we never will, but that is part of their appeal.

SATAN, LAUGHING, SPREADS HIS WINGS

Of course, it goes without saying that while all this was going on the sonic juggernaut that was Black Sabbath continued to trample all in its path. The seminal "Paranoid" single, released in the UK in September 1970 (with the album appearing a month later), pushed the band into the stratospheric heights of rock stardom. Among the other tracks on the album was one of the band's strongest and most memorable pieces, "War Pigs," a song critical of the Vietnam War (which was providing unimaginable horrors of its own). Black Sabbath's chugging doom-laden riffs were in contrast to Led Zeppelin's more fantasy-oriented fare, and they were without doubt one of *the* most influential bands in heavy and occult rock genres, lending a creative springboard to many bands in that decade and beyond. This writer (Simon) would wager that without Black Sabbath, such subgenres as doom, grindcore and sludgecore would never have materialized, or would have done so a lot later on if the band hadn't existed.

Let's not forget that at the beginning of 1975 emerged a band that has possibly the closest link of all to the horror genre—Goblin. This band is mainly known for creating the score for Dario Argent's films, their progressive synthesized soundscapes adding layers of depth to Argento's already disturbing celluloid visions. Although their sound may appear dated to today's ears, there's still something ineffable about the marriage between their music and Argento's imagery. It's a powerful symbiosis, lending a particularly esoteric atmosphere to the films. The formula of cutting-edge giallo filmmaking and electronic rock scores was a winning one, eagerly taken up by others in the Italian horror film industry, with varying degrees of success—or not, as the case may be.

What we've mainly concentrated on here are the highlights of the early part of the decade—undoubtedly there were plenty of obscure rock bands which allied horror to their musical output. The seventies would turn out to be a very interesting decade musically, one which led to an explosion in the music industry and the proliferation of musical projects and bands. In the next installment of this series, we will be dealing with the advent of punk and new wave, and the behemoth which the indie music scene created as a result.

Tune in next time!

John Boden resides in the shadow of Three Mile Island with his wonderful wife and children. Aside from his work with *Shock Totem*, his stories can be found in *52 Stitches, Everyday Weirdness, Black Ink Horror #7,* and *Psychos: Serial Killers, Depraved Madmen, and the Criminally Insane,* edited by **John Skipp**.

Simon Marshall-Jones is a UK-based writer, artist, editor, publisher and blogger: also wine and cheese lover, music freak and covered in too many tattoos.

THE LONG ROAD

by Kristi DeMeester

It'll never leave you, Danny. Not now that you've heard them. Bet you can feel them itching down inside your guts. Bet you can hear them moving around out there at night. Sounds pretty, don't it? Bet it gets your pecker hard just thinking about it." Pop coughed, deep and wet in his chest, spit flecking gray stubble. He fumbled for the glass resting on the end table next to him, gulped at the brackish water he'd pulled from the marsh, smacked his lips and grunted.

"You thirsty, Danny?" he said, offering me the glass. I didn't want to answer him. Because I wanted that water, wanted to take it deep into myself, cool the burning working its way through my belly and down into my groin. But there were things moving in the dark liquid, things made up of shadow and night. Things that bite and tear and eat. I couldn't see them exactly. Could see only the outlines, the hint of fingers—or were they tentacles?—scrabbling, the slight high pitched hum of jagged teeth against glass, and I was afraid of those things burrowing inside of me, eating their way from the inside out. I shook my head.

"Suit yourself," he said.

In the night, I tried not to hear them. The beasts that moved. Long, slow undulations beneath the reeds that made me think of fish whipping their tails. Only there had never been any fish here. Pop dragged Ma here when she was fourteen, her brown skin stretched tight over the seed in her belly, and tied her to this place of rot. It took fifteen years for the beasts to come. They found us and spoke their words, their voices honeyed, and the world turned inside out like an animal peeled out of its skin.

Pop was the first to listen to them. *Walking the long road*, he called it. He took to the water like an alcoholic takes to whiskey, and before long his insides started seeping out of him, his blue eyes turning black and oily. Then Momma disappeared into the night, and the beasts ripped the sky open with their shrieking, and I knew that the Devil moved in that water. It didn't matter how much it burned, how pretty they sang, I wouldn't drink.

My tongue dried against the roof of my mouth, and Pop dragged his finger along the glass, suckled at the last few drops. "You'll walk the road before too long, boy. And they'll be there waiting on you. Sure as shit they'll find you, crawl inside that pretty hide of yours, scratch that itch in your belly. Like the balm of fucking Gilead." And he laughed, his jaw working loose from the skin, the smell of his decay rising, hot and liquid.

And I was moving out the door, letting it bang behind me like the way Momma would have once hollered that I wasn't *raised in a fucking barn, Danny. We got some manners in this family.* Only there was no Momma anymore, and I ran until my calves cramped, and I tumbled into the dirt.

Everywhere was the smell, the hushed whispers, and my skin blistering with the want, the need to drink of them. *This is my body. This is my blood.* The Holy Communion. The wafer and the wine. My body burning from the inside out, their voices scraping and sliding against my skin like claws and teeth hunting meat, but there was sweetness there, too, and the shame when I went hard, the shame when I pressed my body against the earth, spurting helplessly against the dust.

"Hard not to scratch that itch, ain't it, Danny boy," Pop said and moved beside me, knelt before the water, his hands twitching, dancing across the surface as the beasts unfurled, reached toward him. The fingers and hands of lovers.

He grinned. *Like the cat who ate the canary,* Momma would have called it. He had lost his molars, and he brought a finger against his right incisor, pushed and wiggled until the tooth fell into the dirt.

"Reckon I don't need them anymore, huh Danny boy? The pipes are fucking calling, and shouldn't you be dead?" He paused, pushed against the left incisor until it too came loose then tossed it into the water.

"No, not you. But somebody you love. Somebody you love in the cold, cold ground, and you just keep on living, Danny boy. You'll push your lips against her grave and whisper to the worms, and that itch will just keep on gnawing at you." His eyes flickered, the darkness momentarily pulling away from something deeper.

Water leaked from my father's eyes, his mouth, dripped from what remained of his teeth. His lips coated with dark viscous dribbling, and his skin seemed to rattle, loose around his bones. His mouth opened, a great yawning chasm, and I could see the beasts reaching from his throat, groping at his tongue, as if the things inside were trying to find their way out.

"Come on and walk the long road, Danny," he said, and the things inside of him laughed, a deep gurgling that sounded like drowning.

And I ran.

~

I met Sarah ten years later. And while there were miles and years between, at night I'd dream of the long road, the beasts, and the water. Wake up screaming in the darkness, the mattress sweat-soaked and cold.

I'd taken another girl to see Tom Waits. A girl like all of the other girls, the names vanishing as soon as they spoke them. She had spent the night applying and reapplying her too pink lipstick. Every now and again her hand would brush against my crotch. Pathetic attempt at seduction. Her brightly painted face like something you could look through and see the broken parts. Buried things she covered with the sharpness of her hipbones, with the emptiness of her sex.

I told her I needed a cigarette, left her sitting there, frowning at her own reflection mirrored in a lavender compact as she checked her lipstick once more.

Vanity made flesh, and I moved away from her, through the sea of people into the spring night air that did not smell of salt but of pine.

Sarah was sitting on the curb, a dark sweater pulled tightly around her shoulders, the tip of her cigarette just barely illuminating the angles of her face. She looked frail, birdlike, as if I could gather her into my arms and grind her bones into dust. Her hair was cut short then, dark spikes tipped with crimson, the only color against her pale, clear face. She would tell me later that makeup made her feel like she was staring at the world from behind a mask, like what people saw was not really her but some approximation of her, a thing walking around in Sarah skin.

"So what are you running from?" Her voice startled me. I'd expected something light and airy, a voice to match the delicacy of her body, but the sound was deep and gruff. A voice steeped in long years of whiskey and cigarettes.

"I'm not running from anything."

She turned to face me. Dark eyes framed by tangled lashes. "That's bullshit, brother."

"Guess I could ask you the same question."

She inhaled sharply, laughed. "The same thing you are."

"I doubt that."

"See? So you do admit it," she said and stood. She was taller than I thought she would be, and she crossed her arms over her chest. It was a protective gesture that prevented physical closeness. Much time would pass before she would unfold herself, and even then, her arms would be hard, her embraces too tight as if reminding herself that *Yes, this is real, I have accepted this moment.*

We both went quiet then, smoked our cigarettes in the darkness.

"See you around," she said, flicked her cigarette into the bushes, and began a slow walk back to the building.

"What's your name?" I called after her.

"Sarah," she said, and waved a hand in farewell, her slight form suddenly swallowed up. It took me two days to work up the courage to try to find her, try to figure out who she was, where she belonged.

She owned a florist's shop over on Midland Avenue, a small building of crumbling brick that I'd passed often enough to know the sign. I spent another three days driving past it, telling myself each time that I would stop, would go inside and talk with her, but I would speed by, afraid she would see me and think I was some creep.

Fucking do it, Danny. Just stop the goddamn car and walk inside. Tell her that you want to know her, tell her that you can't stop thinking about the things she said, tell her that you want to take her to dinner, to coffee, anything...

Thoughts bumping against themselves, and my blood throbbing at my temples when I finally worked up the courage to go into the shop. Hoping she could be the thing to help me forget the house, the water, the beasts at the end of that long road.

"Looks like you aren't running away after all," she said, a small stone glinting in the curve of her nose. I hadn't noticed it before.

I swallowed and told her the thing I'd been practicing for the past week. "Maybe it isn't running away. Maybe it's just taken me all this time to figure out what I was running to."

"You're fucking kidding me with that line, right?" she said and narrowed her eyes, but there was a smile curling at the edges of her lips, and I dipped my head, tried not to grin.

She taught me the names of flowers, my tongue tripping over the syllables, and at night when we lay in bed together I told her the stories locked in my head, the ones I knew by heart but was afraid to write down.

"You should do something with these, Danny," she said and pressed a hand against my chest.

"Maybe one day." Only I knew that I would never put them to paper. If I did, the world would come undone by its strings, and I'd be fifteen and on the long road again with Pop standing over me, his body dripping into the dirt.

"I'm serious. You're too talented to be stuck writing ad copy for some shitty, small time roofer."

"Maybe one day," I repeated, but then her mouth was on mine, and her lips tasted of honeysuckle and wine, and for a long while, I lost myself in the movements of her body.

When the nightmares took me, she didn't speak, didn't move until I came back to the world.

She only asked me about them once. "What are they? You talk about them in your sleep."

"It's nothing," I told her, and she pursed her lips, nodded. She had her secrets, too. A mother she never mentioned. An expired bottle of anti-hallucinogens tucked deep inside her bedside table drawer. A long vertical scar on her right wrist.

She filled my bedroom with flowers, and underneath the nightmare smells of salt and decay, the Carolina jasmine breathed its perfume into the night air, and slowly, slowly, the nightmares began to recede. The beasts becoming nothing more than shadowy figures, incorporeal wisps compared to Sarah's sleeping form, her breath warm against my chest. My childhood shrinking against what we called love.

Six months in, I wrapped a key to my place in an old watch box, lit some candles, opened a bottle of wine. She opened the box slowly, her fingers tracing the key's jagged outlines, her face expressionless.

"I'm sorry. It's too fast. Is it too fast? Just so you can get in if I'm not here, you know? You don't have to use it if you don't want to."

"Would you shut up for a second?" She lifted the key from the box, a momentary flashing of silver, and closed her hand around it.

"If you suddenly morph into some asshole, I'm cleaning this place out and selling all your shit on eBay," she said, and I brought her hand to my mouth, pressed my lips to her fingers.

"Never."

She bought a delicate silver chain and wore the key around her neck; the metal nestled in the hollow of her throat.

"You shouldn't wear it there. Some weirdo could see it and follow you back here," I told her.

"You would protect me."

"Great. Have you seen me, Sarah? They'd probably rape me first."

"I like wearing it. The heaviness of it. It reminds me of you. Lets me know it's real."

It took another six months to save for a ring—a fleck of diamond in a thin gold band.

"It's a beautiful ring. She's a damn lucky gal," the saleswoman said and smiled, winking an eye smeared with one too many layers of kohl black eyeliner.

I told her we were going hiking. "Supposed to be the best weekend for fall color," I said against her protestations. There was a small mountain to climb, and when we crested the top, our breath coming quick and shallow, I gave her the ring.

"It doesn't fit," she said against her laughter.

"We can fix it," I said, and she pulled me deep into the forest, away from the trail. The smell of pine lingered in her hair for days afterward.

But then winter came and the nights grew long, cold, and she began to vanish inside of herself. It was like watching her disappear, like watching her become a ghost.

In January she stopped sleeping. She would lie in the dark with me, match her breathing to mine until I fell asleep. But when I would wake in the night, covered in the hard sweat of dreams, she would be gone, the place where her body should be cold.

I could hear her moving about on the roof above me, whispering to the stars, telling the faceless gods her secrets as she chain smoked, the cigarettes burning down to the tips of her fingers.

"It's nothing. I'll put some ointment on it," she said, when I saw the burns. But each night she would leave me, find her way onto the roof, her voice floating down to me, words cut from nightmares.

"They found me once, when I was a girl," she told me one night in late January. There was snow, a light dusting of white over hard ground. "They came crawling out of the walls, made nests in my hair."

"What found you?"

"Can't you see them, Danny?" she asked, and her voice reminded me of Pop's, of the deep gurgling of the beasts, and I had the sudden desire to wrap my hands around her throat, to make her choke on the words she offered up like holy baubles.

"There's nothing there," I said, but she shook her head, turned from me and moaned.

"They come out of the walls. Mother always said they come out of the walls. They want my skin, Danny. They want my skin."

I took her to the doctor, watched her as she took the pills he prescribed. But night after night, I could hear her moving above me.

"They won't leave," she whispered, and I held her tight, her bones like knives threatening to cut through her tissue-paper skin.

When she split open the old scar, peeled back her flesh to let the things step inside of her, I found her too late, her blood blooming around her like the flowers she loved.

And I buried her, screamed what I had known was love against the frozen earth. *Old Danny Boy and his fucking pipes are calling.*

~

Sarah has been dead for two weeks, and I am on the long road. It's certain what I will find waiting for me when I reach the end of it, and I listen for the beasts to begin their singing. Seems like I was always headed back here.

The old itch starts up in my belly, and from under the water, the beasts move, the smell of salt and decay thick in the air. I do not think of Sarah, only of the itch that needs scratching.

Pop is waiting for me in the house at the end of the long road. And when I get there, I'll take the glass of water he gives me. I have been walking for a long while, and I am so thirsty.

Kristi DeMeester lives, loves, and writes in Atlanta where she also serves as the fiction editor at *Loose Change* magazine. Her work has appeared or is forthcoming in *Shimmer, Daily Science Fiction, Niteblade*, and *Every Day Fiction* among others. Growing up both Southern and Pentecostal, she witnessed travelling preachers cast out demons. These demons still haunt her writing.

Please visit her at www.oneperfectword.blogspot.com.

Stargazer Breech and Choking
A CONVERSATION WITH VIOLET LEVOIT

by John Boden

Violet Glaze, aka Violet LeVoit. Renegade wielder of words as weapons. Not sleek, shiny words like razors or flip-knives, scary intimidating language like a knotted caveman club with dried brains and hair stuck to it. This woman writes shit that boggles the mind.

The first exposure I had to her work was via John Skipp's *Werewolves and Shapeshifters* anthology and her wonderful story, "Warm, In Your Coat." Then upon meeting Skipp in person at Necon 2011 and talking new blood, he must have dropped her name no less than six times.

Skipp released her first collection, the uncompromisingly titled *I Am Genghis Cum*, on his own Fungasm Books, which is an imprint of Eraserhead Press. With a title like that I was expecting some hardcore bizarro shenanigans. LeVoit delivered. She didn't lull me in with pretty prose and sneaky emotional foreplay. She kicked in my door, grabbed the book from my hands, and proceeded to shove it down my throat. She is unrelenting. There are no easy outs; her fiction just punches straight through.

Recently I was fortunate to get to chew the proverbial fat with the lovely Ms. LeVoit, which went a little bit like this.

~

JB: Would you mind painting a little back-story for me, as to how a nice girl like you ended up slinging such vicious wordage at the masses? Your style is so insanely sharp and daring, I've really not read anything like it before.

VL: Wow, thanks for thinking I'm a nice girl. Here's some theories how I got this way: I was born stargazer breech and choking on my own umbilical cord, in Baltimore, City of the Inbred Undead, stomping grounds of John Waters, Frank Zappa, Edgar Allan Poe and Madalyn Murray O'Hair. I had a perfectly delightful childhood where no one tried to bury me in the backyard, but through genetic luck o' the draw I got a brain that was, shall we say, more deluxe than most. It's full of delights, like synesthesia and lucid dreams, but I've also struggled with mental illness in lots of delicious flavors since the age of nine. The cherry on top was being in labor for 90 hours during the birth of my son. That'll PTSD you up real good.

(People ask how women end up as horror writers—as if, shouldn't we be writing romances whilst ironing?—but to me, if you're born with a body that conspires to kill you, either by bloodletting, or childbirth, or being cancerously poisoned from a lifetime of percolating hormones, how are most women not horror writers?)

The other thing about me is that I'm not actually a writer. All my formal training (until recently) was in fine arts, and I think that's how my brain is still primarily oriented. I'm a painter who types.

Beyond that, I've got no idea why I can't write Nice Literary Fiction About Dismayed White People. It all comes out vomit and werewolves.

JB: John Skipp is a big waver of the LeVoit banner. I've met the man and he is golden. How did you first meet him? Was the *Werewolves* story a blind submission and the rest is history?

VL: Actually, I was lucky enough to be introduced to John through my comrade Mikita Brottman. She's an author and educator specializing in the horrific aspects of American culture, and we share a lot of the same dark sensibilities. I would run into her at film screenings in Baltimore (I'm also a film critic) and we immediately hit it off, because how can you not love a woman who's curated a book about the cultural significance of car crashes? She suggested I send that "Warm, In Your Coat" story you loved on to John. So I agree, the man is golden, and if it wasn't for him I wouldn't have known I'd been writing "bizarro" all this time. John's the guy who generously took my self-published manuscript of *I Am Genghis Cum* and spun it into the expanded Fungasm Press edition you're so smitten with.

(While we're on the subject, Mikita's got two new horror books worth checking out: *House of Quiet Shadows*, published under John Skipp's Ravenous Shadows imprint; and *Thirteen Girls*, which is one of the bleakest, saddest, most un-put-down-able books about serial killer aftermath I've ever read.)

JB: It may not be proper etiquette, but I don't care—you have submitted several stories to *Shock Totem*, and while they have not been right for us because we don't really deal in "bizarro," they have all been so crazy. I've loved them. Your ideas are just off the charts. Your style has a certain stream of consciousness sort of vibe. Is that how writing is for you? Do you just turn the valve a bit and let it go?

VL: You know when you get cotton candy at the fair? They turn on the machine and the perforated drum walls get all fuzzy fiberglass flossy, but it's not until they dip that paper cone that it spools into a thick sticky treat for you. Writing's like that for me. My brain spins invisible ideas but I can't tell they're there until there's something hard for them to catch on. The story comes out quickly as a series of scenes, at least up to the second act. I quickly scribble down the scenes, not as a draft but as beats to hit, and in the process of filling out those scenes the third act becomes visible.

For example, one day I was thinking about the trendiness of geographic names for girls—Paris, Brooklyn, Dakota. You know what's a beautiful name that'll never catch on? Treblinka. And suddenly I knew who would get named Treblinka, and the first two acts of the story spun out as "When the Zoos Close Down They'll Come for Us," which is included in the new John Skipp-edited *Psychos* anthology from Black Dog & Leventhal.

Sometimes I dream entire stories and all I have to do is scribble the plot down in the morning. "Rough Trade Marks the Spot" in *I Am Genghis Cum* was born that way. It feels like I'm cheating when I do that.

I took advice from Roald Dahl, who insisted that when you get an inspiration you must write it down immediately, even if it means squeaking out some words with your finger in the grime on your car. He's absolutely right about that. Good ideas don't wait.

JB: How important is music to what you do? I find it obvious to references in your stories to the fact that I saw you robbed of the title at Necon karaoke with a wonderful rendition of "Bizarre Love Triangle." You've got a voice! Have you done the music thing before?

VL: I love, love, LOVE to sing. It's the one talent I vowed I'll only do for love and not money. So the next time you're on some file-sharing site and you find something either from Violet LeVoit or my noise-electronica project Vanishing Twin, feel free to download.

JB: What is on the glorious horizon?

VL: Graphic novels. I've partnered with illustrator Greg Houston to do an idea we've been kicking around for some time about Johnny Eck, the Baltimore-born sideshow performer who can be seen in the movie *Freaks*. He was born with no body below the navel, so he ambulated on his hands like R2-D2. He was a good-looking guy, too. He's sort of my Baltimore dream date. Any man who ends at the fourth rib has got to be good at other things.

JB: Freaks is an all-time favorite of mine. Well, I just want to say thanks so much for your time!

VL: You're the best, John. And one of these days I vow I'll have something for *Shock Totem* readers to devour.

Thing In a Bag

by M. Bennardo

Thompson shifted his weight from one foot to the other as he stood before the bulletin board in the Nashville Greyhound station. He hated, hated, hated it when things went bad. It was only partly because he was out the money, and only partly because all the work was for nothing. Mostly it was the queasy nervous feeling he got in places like this. It was the waiting, the interminable waiting. He was bored and keyed up at the same time.

At least none of the photocopies on the board looked familiar. They were all kidnappers and rapists. What a hick town. What a filthy stupid hick town that would let kidnappers and rapists get away, but would stake out an honest little outfit like his.

Thompson felt bad about leaving the rest of the gang behind, but that bug hadn't just found its own way into Carl's apartment. One of them had talked. This was the only way—a quiet getaway before the gang or the cops knew anything about it. By the time somebody else asked where he was, he'd be halfway to wherever he was going. Thompson checked his ticket again. Charlotte. Another hick town probably, but the quickest way out of Nashville.

How long before the cops showed up? How long before they started asking: Have you seen this guy? Flashing a surveillance picture of him. Have you seen this guy? The guy at the ticket counter would scratch his head. Not sure, he'd say. When did he come through? The cops would shrug. Wednesday probably. Tuesday maybe. The guy at the ticket counter would scratch his head again. Well, I don't know, he'd say. Nobody on Wednesday, I don't think. But there was this one guy on Tuesday.

Thompson suppressed the urge to kick a trash can. There was nothing he could do now to stop himself from becoming this one guy on Tuesday. Yeah, the ticket guy would say. Yeah now that I'm thinking about it I'm pretty sure he did come through here. It was probably around eight o'clock on Tuesday night. I think he got on the Charlotte bus but let me just check the schedule here.

Thompson stalked into the main terminal and slumped down on a bench. He already looked suspicious enough, going to Charlotte with no luggage. Better sit down. Better just keep his head down until he could get on the bus. He could think on the bus—think about how to get back to New York. And sleep. Right now he needed to look normal. He needed just to fit in.

There was a big bag on the seat next to Thompson, the kind that sailors carry. But somebody picked up that bag and shifted it one seat over and moved over next to Thompson. Great. Here came a conversation. Thompson looked straight ahead, didn't even glance at the other guy. Just looked across at the white tile wall while the gas fumes tickled his nose. He sneezed.

"Gesundheit," said the other guy.

"Thanks," said Thompson, wiping his nose with his sleeve. He still didn't look at the other guy. He tried to look like a loser. He tried to look like the kind of guy nobody would want to talk to.

"You got a cigarette?" asked the other guy.

Thompson shook his head. "No." He really didn't. He could feel the guy hovering over him. Maybe he hadn't heard. Thompson turned to look at him. He was a middle-aged guy with thinning red hair, a big nose, and watery blue eyes. He looked thin and shaky, like he was a drug addict. Or maybe he used to be one. "No, sorry," said Thompson again.

The other guy slid his hand smoothly up to his ear and pulled a cigarette out from behind it. "Gotta save this one," he said matter of factly. "It's a good one too." The guy reached over to the bag on the seat next to him and opened the top and fiddled for a couple seconds. When he sat back down again, he had one cigarette between his lips and the other one back behind his ear again. "And these ones ain't any good," he said, trying to get a spark on a lighter. "They smoke all right, but they taste terrible." He lit the cigarette and took a puff. "I'd offer you one," he said, "but you gotta smoke 'em fast." He took another long draw, and then coughed into his hand. "Name's Bates."

Thompson just nodded.

"You got a name?" asked Bates.

Thompson wanted to look away or stand up and leave or smack the guy. But he couldn't look suspicious. As long as there was a chance he'd get away, he had to sit there and take it. Thompson tried to think of a name.

"Hey, you!" came a call from the other side of the terminal. It was the guy at the ticket counter. "Bag man!" he shouted. "Bag man, there ain't no smoking in here!"

Bates shrugged and dropped the cigarette. "Was about to go bad anyway," he muttered, as he ground it out with his shoe. It left a sticky pink streak where he'd mashed it with his heel. Bates just giggled a little. "Oops."

"Call me Custer," said Thompson.

"All right," said Bates. "You're Custer."

~

The bus to Charlotte was mostly empty. It had been dark a few hours by the time it pulled out, and Thompson felt dumber than ever not having any luggage with him. But it would have been even dumber to go back to his hotel to get his stuff.

The night was getting chilly, so Thompson hunted out a seat near a warm air vent and hunched down, hugging himself. He only had a thin jacket on, and he figured it was going to get a lot colder when they got to the mountains. The bus driver walked back down the aisle, checking every seat as he went. He stopped where Bates was sitting, a row ahead of Thompson. "You gotta put that bag up," said the bus driver.

"Yes, sir," Thompson heard Bates say. "Yes, I will surely do that in a minute."

The bus driver walked to the back of the bus and back down toward the front. He stopped at Bates again. "I said you gotta put that bag up."

"I will surely do it in just a minute," said Bates.

"What you got in there, anyway?"

"Meteorite. Crashed right in my front yard."

The bus driver grunted. "Just put it away," he said. "Whatever it is, just put it away."

"Yes, right away," said Bates. He stood up in the aisle as the driver moved away, and suddenly shot Thompson a look. Thompson couldn't tell why, but the hair on the back of his neck stood up as Bates winked. Then he sat down again, the bag still on the seat next to him.

~

Thompson woke a few hours later. He'd been sleeping with his forehead against the window, and now his nose was numb and his neck was stiff. Outside it was pitch black. The lights Thompson could see looked blurry and indistinct, and a couple seconds later he realized why. There was thick snow swirling in front of the window, coming down quiet and hard. It was then that Thompson realized the bus had stopped. One thing was sure, this wasn't Charlotte.

The bus driver stood up and leaned over the back of his seat. "Well, folks," he said. "You can see we got some snow here. My dispatcher is telling me it's a lot worse up around Knoxville, and they are recommending we don't head into the mountains until morning." There was a general groaning from the other passengers at this. "We're pulled into a truck stop here, and there's a diner across the parking lot if you want to get anything to eat. There's a motel a little bit further on, but otherwise I'm gonna be leaving the bus running all night. But if you got any blankets or coats, I'd suggest you get them out."

Thompson shivered. He hugged himself tighter, and rolled up in a ball next to the window. He'd be even later getting into Charlotte and he still had no idea what he was going to do when he got there. They might even have his poster up on the board by then. It all depended on how late they were, and how soon the cops missed him, and—well, it just depended on so many things out of his control.

"Hey," said somebody. "Hey, Custer!" Thompson didn't remember at first that was supposed to be him. Somebody jogged his arm. "Hey, Custer." It was Bates.

"What is it?"

"You want to split some dinner and a room?" Bates had pulled on a flannel jacket from somewhere, and was standing in the aisle with his bag hanging down his back.

"I don't got that much cash," said Thompson. "I wasn't expecting to have to stay overnight."

"You got twenty bucks?" asked Bates. "You got twenty bucks, or ten bucks? That's all we need. Just trust me."

Thompson tried to wave him off. "I just want to get some sleep."

"Get some in a bed," said Bates. "Come on, just trust me. It won't cost you anything."

~

"So where you come from?" asked Bates, between bites of his hamburger. "You ain't from Tennessee."

Thompson was picking the tomatoes off his club sandwich. "I don't like to talk about myself."

Bates cackled. "A man buys you dinner, the least you can do is answer a question."

"You haven't bought it yet."

"Don't you worry about it," said Bates. "Just trust me."

Thompson smashed a triangle of toast back down on a tomato-free sandwich. A spurt of mayonnaise dribbled out the side and down the stack of turkey. "I should have stayed on the bus," he said. "I feel like you're mixing me up in something."

Bates spread his hands, holding out a shoestring fry in one of them. "I ain't getting you mixed up in anything. I'm just buying a man dinner." Bates bent over and started loosening the laces on his bag.

"I'm from up north," said Thompson.

Bates giggled again. "I can tell that. What are you doing down here?"

Thompson shoved a couple of fries in his mouth and grunted. "Leaving."

Bates had the bag open now and dropped a fry down inside. He tried to do it nonchalant, but the casual air only made Thompson take all the more notice of it. Bates followed the first fry with a couple more.

"What are you doing? Saving them for later?"

Bates stowed the bag under the table again. "Something like that."

"What's in there?" asked Thompson.

"A leprechaun. Found him wriggling in a raccoon trap in my front yard."

Thompson chewed a strip of bacon from his club sandwich. "All right then," he said. "You got your secrets, and I got mine."

"Sure, sure," said Bates. He drained the last of his milkshake and picked up the check. "I'm gonna get a few biscuits to go and take care of this." Thompson just nodded as he chewed. Bates held out his hand. "You got that twenty dollar bill?"

"I thought you were buying."

Bates picked up his bag and hugged it under his arm. "You'll get it back. Trust me."

"I'll be watching you," said Thompson. Much as he felt like a chump, he wanted to see what Bates's game was. Maybe he'd even learn some new angle. "Don't forget we're gonna be on the same bus again in the morning."

Bates walked up to the register in front and set the bag down on the floor. He wasn't so close anymore, but Thompson almost thought he could see something moving in the bottom of that bag, and for the second time his hair stood on end. Whatever was in there, he didn't like it. He didn't like Bates much either.

Thompson could see Bates talking up the girl at the register, and then getting a couple of biscuits wrapped to go. Then Bates bent down and seemed to slip the twenty dollar bill into the bag. It only took a second, and then he stood up again and handed it over to the girl. Thompson swore under his breath. The only angle he'd learned was not to give money to strangers from the Greyhound. He thought about jumping up before Bates could get out the door, but instead he just seethed. He couldn't afford to make a scene, and he had eaten the dinner. He was just a chump, that was all.

But then Bates cinched up the bag and strolled back to the table, waving the twenty dollar bill in the air with a pleased grin on his face. Thompson sat up, his mouth wide. What had that been about? Some kind of sleight of hand? Wouldn't the girl at the register have noticed? Bates sure didn't seem to be any big hurry to get out.

"I'll give it back when we get to the motel," said Bates. "I'll probably need it there." Thompson kept his eye on the girl at the register as he followed Bates out, but she didn't do anything except wave as they stepped out into the snowy night. If she was missing twenty bucks, she sure hadn't noticed yet.

~

Thompson eyed Bates's long, prone form on the bed in the motel room and listened. It was a tiny room with just a single bed—that would be an interesting argument come lights out—but it had cost them sixty bucks just the same. Bates had done the same weird sleight of hand at the motel check in, and even though Thompson had watched him closely, he still couldn't figure it out. He swore he saw three twenties come out of the bag, and then after they'd locked the room door, Bates had given him back his twenty. It looked the same. Thompson couldn't figure the angle—either that bag was full of terrible cigarettes and twenty dollar bills, or it really was a leprechaun.

It looked like Bates was asleep, but Thompson waited to hear a hitch in his breathing to be sure. He doubted that Bates had meant to sleep yet—he'd just lain down after taking off his shoes and had seemed to drift off suddenly. But Thompson wasn't really interested in Bates exactly. He was interested in the bag, now lying on the floor against the bed.

Suddenly, Bates murmured and brushed his mouth with his hand. He was fully gone now. Thompson carefully picked up the bag and moved it over to the room's tiny table. He didn't dare turn on the light. He didn't dare leave the room either—which would have been the safer course—in case Bates were to wake and miss his precious bag.

This was the first time that Thompson had touched the bag, and a wave of revulsion came over him as he handled it. It felt ropey and a little spongy, like a bag full of sausages. But worse. It was a little warm and oddly heavy. Thompson remembered playing games when he was a kid—sticking his hand into a box and somebody telling him it was guts or eyeballs, but really it was just spaghetti or grapes. Handling the bag he felt almost the same way, and had to work hard not to throw it back down again.

Just before setting it down on the table, Thompson could have sworn it jerked in his hands. He stood back and watched it for a minute, but it didn't move again. He sneaked a glance at Bates. Still asleep, so far as he could tell. If he wanted to look inside, this was the time.

The contents were about the size of a basketball, and were all down at the very bottom of the bag. Thompson had to reach down past a lot of canvas before he got to the thing inside. The first time he put his hand in to pull it out, he instantly lost his nerve. So he pulled it back out again and opened the top wider. He wanted to have a look at the thing.

A sweet smell wafted out of the bag, tinged with a bit of sourness. It was like the smell of apples going bad. Or maybe apples and ground beef. Thompson covered his mouth and looked away until the smell dissipated a bit. He picked up a pen from the table and started lifting aside the folds of the bag. Finally he spied something down in the dark, but couldn't quite make out what it was. What he could see of it was red and purple, and was like something out of a person— something like guts or brains. Thompson was sure he could see it slowly throbbing. He reached in with the pen and prodded it.

The point of the pen made a little depression in the thing, but when he pulled it back it started to fill in again. Suddenly something tumbled out of the bag, and Thompson stepped back swiftly, jamming his knuckle in between his teeth to keep from shouting. But when the object dropped to the floor, he could see it was just another pen. Thompson looked at the pen, at the thing in the bag, and at Bates. He didn't dare move an inch. But then Bates murmured again and let out a long half-snoring sigh. Thompson exhaled slowly.

Thompson inched the pen forward with the toe of his shoe, and it rolled across the carpet into the light. It looked exactly like the pen from the motel. Thompson bent down and picked it up with his sleeve covering his fingers, then set it down on the table. It felt like a pen, and moved like a pen when he poked it.

When he touched it with his fingers, it had the same cool metal feel as a pen. He picked it up and clicked the button. A tip protruded. Thompson looked for a piece of paper and scribbled a bit. It wrote like a pen too.

Thompson reached into his pocket and dug around for some change. When he found a quarter, he reached that down into the bag and touched it to the thing. It gave a little spasm, and a second later, a quarter rolled out of the bag. Thompson tried a couple more times, and soon he had three quarters in addition to the one he'd taken out of his pocket. He jingled them quietly in his cupped hands, and it felt the same as jingling quarters always felt. The right weight, the right coolness, the right clink as they hit each other. The only odd thing was that they all looked exactly the same—same date on the obverse, same scratch on the back. Perfect copies.

Thompson took one of the new quarters and impulsively bit it. It felt hard like metal, but tasted terrible—the same sweet and sour pungency he'd smelled when he first opened the bag. Trying not to gag, Thompson bit it hard again. This time he could feel his teeth sink a little into the coin. When he took the quarter out of his mouth again, he could see little teeth marks in a neat semi-circle across both sides. Underneath the bite marks, pale pink showed through. Not a perfect copy, then. A good copy. Good enough to get them dinner and a motel room at least.

Thompson set the coins all down on the table and glanced toward Bates with a different look in his eyes. That bag would be a useful thing to have—especially until the heat blew over. Thompson looked thoughtfully around the room. Bed, table, lamp, clock, television. This wasn't the kind of place to have an iron. Thompson lifted the lamp, tested it in his hand. That would have to do. He put it back down and unplugged it.

Bates murmured and stirred on the bed as Thompson leaned over him. Then suddenly he gave a single loud snort and his eyelids popped open, those watery irises staring up in surprise. Bates sat up swiftly in bed, but Thompson and his lamp moved just as swiftly to stop him.

~

Thompson dabbed at the cut above his eye with wet toilet paper. It didn't look too deep, but it would probably swell up by morning. That would look suspicious on the bus. Especially if he left with Bates and then came back alone. Well, he just wouldn't get on the bus again. Now that he had that thing—whatever it was—he didn't need to go to Charlotte at all. He'd go someplace else entirely. But first—first he had to get rid of Bates's bag.

The thing was still sitting on the tabletop where Thompson had left it. It didn't seem to move much—it just sat there, pulsing or twitching occasionally. Thompson reached for the pen again, but then pulled his hand away as it dissolved into pink goo at his touch. That must have been the fake. The copy. The quarters were disintegrating too—so it seemed that ten minutes or so was about the limit of how long these copies would last.

Thompson wiped his fingers off on his jeans and then picked up the real pen. Carefully, he lifted the last fold of the bag off the thing and saw that the rest of it was just as repulsive as the part he'd already seen. Thompson grimaced as he looked it over. He wondered just where exactly Bates had gotten an ugly thing like that.

Remembering how Bates had fed the thing French fries, Thompson unwrapped one of the biscuits they'd brought over from the restaurant. It had mimicked a few twenty dollar bills, a pen, and some change since then—if the thing really did eat, then it might be hungry now. Thompson broke off a bit of biscuit and tossed it at the thing.

At first, nothing happened. The biscuit crumbs fell onto it and seemed to start soaking up some of the moisture from the thing's skin, but otherwise that was it. It was only gradually that Thompson realized the crumbs weren't soaking up moisture—the thing was soaking up the crumbs, pulling them in through its skin. By the time Thompson understood what was happening, they were almost entirely consumed.

Thompson broke off a bigger chunk of biscuit and held it out to the thing. When he got close, the thing's skin distended and reached out a little, sucking at the biscuit. Thompson pulled back, and the biscuit came apart in his fingers, half of it sucked away. Watching the biscuit fade into the guts of the thing, Thompson thought it was odd how it didn't mimic the food and how it didn't suck on the pen or the coins.

By way of experiment, Thompson poked it with the pen again and for the first time could see clearly the replica pen budding off the side of the thing. A bump rose up like a submarine rising from the ocean depths and then seemed to swirl in on itself—growing longer and thinner. It lifted out quickly and then hardened into the pen again and dropped off onto the tabletop. Instead of picking it up, Thompson just pushed it back into the thing with his finger and felt the suction start.

Then suddenly Thompson was caught by a movement in the corner of his eye. Rising up out of the back of the thing, furthest from him, was a wiggling appendage about four inches long, waving back and forth like a tiny pink snake. Thompson felt his blood run cold, and then suddenly he laughed.

His own finger had pushed the pen all the way back inside, and was now touching the skin of the thing itself. He poked the thing again with his finger, and another wiggling finger rose up at the back of it. It was creepy and disgusting, those disembodied fingers, but it struck Thompson funny too.

Thompson opened a pillowcase and reached out to pick up the thing. It was cool and a little moist to the touch, like a clammy hand, and he'd barely gotten a good grip underneath it when he realized he was touching a clammy hand. The whole section he'd enclosed in his fingers had shifted into a hand just like his own and was gripping him back. Thompson twisted his wrist, looking at the sides and back of the hand he now held in his own. It was just like his—same freckles and everything. It gave him the creeps, and suddenly he wanted only to shake it loose.

But that wasn't so easy. The hand hung on tight. Thompson tried shaking it off, but it was like some wet mass of dough clinging to his fingers. He swore under his breath, looking around for something to scrape it off with. Not seeing anything, he shook his hand again and was surprised when flecks of blood spattered his face. Looking closer, Thompson could see blood running along the seams where the thing touched his own flesh—and now he could also see the fingers on the thing's hand growing thicker and longer as his own sank deeper inside it.

Thompson swore again, and then suddenly the pain hit him, shooting up his forearm to his elbow. He fell to his knees, and tried clubbing the thing against the tabletop, but already his arm felt like a lead weight. There was a buzzing in his brain, and sweat rolled down his temples.

What the hell was happening? It felt like he was being smothered and his hand felt like it was being sucked off his wrist. He couldn't even see his arm anymore—his field of vision was shrinking and everything was out of focus. Something hit the back of Thompson's head and he thought it might have been the back of the chair. And then that was it.

~

Bates was slow in coming to his senses again. Once he did, it took him even longer to realize he was tied up somewhere and then ages to pick the knots in the electrical cords around his wrists and ankles. All he knew was that he needed to get free before he suffocated to death. But then all at once his arms were full of pumping blood and he was tearing the blanket from off his face and kicking open the closet door and taking in deep gulping breaths.

Bloody and fuddled, Bates crawled out of the closet and dragged himself to his feet. He tried to take a step and almost fell over. He'd forgotten his ankles were still tied. Good thing the room was small, he thought wryly to himself, as he practically fell into the chair closest to him. Bates ran his hand through his hair and felt the bloody place. It was scabbing up okay, but it hurt like crazy. That was his own fault, he guessed. His own fault for showing off to a stranger.

Bates picked up his bag from the tabletop and saw immediately it was empty. Of course it was, and that Custer fool was gone too. He'd never see either of them again, of course. Bates collapsed back in his chair and threw the bag across the table onto the other chair. As he bent down to untie his ankles, he wondered how much the other fellow had figured out about the thing. It wasn't the kind of thing you could go messing around with. You were liable to get yourself—

Bates sat up, a cold sweat suddenly breaking across his face and arms. It suddenly struck him that there'd only been one chair in the room. Now there were two—and worse yet, he was sitting in one of them. But which one? Bates shut his eyes and took a deep breath.

"Well," he said. "Only one way to find out." And suddenly pushing both his arms and legs like four coiled springs, he gave it one good shot to get out of that chair.

M. Bennardo's short stories appear in *Three-Lobed Burning Eye*, *Beneath Ceaseless Skies*, and *Asimov's Science Fiction*, among others. He is also editor of the Machine of Death series of anthologies—the second volume, *This Is How You Die*, is coming from Grand Central Publishing in July 2013. He lives in Cleveland, Ohio, but people everywhere can find him online at www.mbennardo.com.

HOWLING THROUGH THE KEYHOLE

The stories behind the stories.

"Consumption"

My sister says I feel too much, and she's right. I have an over-abundance of emotion about all sorts of trivial and inconsequential things. When I'm in good sorts, when my mind is healthy and chemically balanced, I can easily override this excess of feeling with logic, like a master Vulcan. But minds are not always healthy, and when my brain chemistry falls out of balance, so does my rationality.

It is the greatest horror in my life to be trapped by my unreasonable mind. To understand, on some level, the complete nonsense of what I am feeling, and still, to be defenseless against it. It is a battle I fight every day of my life, with anti-depressants and therapy and diet and exercise and all sorts of new-fangled, promising cure-alls. It is a battle I struggle with, but also, for now, one I am winning.

This story is about someone who is losing. She is trapped, not by her relationship, or society, or the apparently disintegrating world around her, but by her own emotions, her own mind. She also feels too much. Those feelings chase each other around in her head until she is so deep inside herself she cannot defend herself against the creature inside her.

Even as she is surrounded by signs that this too shall pass, like the abandoned hospital and the ever-evolving forest, she cannot find release

from the present. Even as she understands the insignificance of her life in the universe, identifying the two people closest to her only as variables, she cannot ignore the weight of her own existence. Even as she obsesses over Y, the story is not about him. He does not consume her. Instead, her desire cannibalizes.

I present this story, not as a representation of mental illness, but as an expression of it. Something from the depths of my own uncontrollable mind. Catharsis to ensure I, and others like me, will wish for longer forevers.

—Victoria Jakes

"Among the Elephants"

"Among the Elephants" is a short story that plays very close to my heart. I wrote it with both my mother and grandmother in mind. Just as the story's character remarks, my own mother "really did work with elephants". Her three ladies, she called them; and she really did introduce me to them by telling me not to be afraid—their respect for her would be the only protection I needed. We fed them Nutter-Butter cookies—which may have been their *real* only reason for putting up with me.

It's my grandmother, Emily, who filled my head with stories of Africa and "places that remembered the world before there were people." The two of them—my two ladies—and the way they've moved through their lives were very much in my mind when I wrote this story of deformity and perseverance. I walk in some very impressive footsteps.

–Amberle L. Husbands

"The Four Horsemen of the Parking Lot"

This piece was written in February 2007. I'm happy to report Neveah is now six years old, and her out-of-the-gate stumble has not held her back. She recently received an orange belt in Karate.

–Kurt Newton

"The Gates of Emile Plimpkin: The Gravedigger's Legacy"

Writers are always asked, "Where do you get your ideas?" This is a standard textbook question, and the asker is usually treated to a standard textbook (wiseacre) remark from the author. A snide reference to an idea shop in Burbank, or, "Who comes up with ideas? I steal 'em."

The truth is, if you're a writer, when you aren't writing you're at least thinking about writing. Thus we're constantly on the lookout for unconnected things which might be strung together. When we have disagreements with our significant others, in the backs of our heads we are mentally recording the more colorful jibes and wish for a notepad to take it all down because we might be able to

use some of the more choice bits later. While on vacation, we enjoy ourselves, and yet we still take stock of the scenery and try to decide how best to work the exotic local into a story. Whether it's a snippet of conversation, a news story, or some factoid read on the net, it's all grist for the mill.

The other thing non-writers wonder is, "Do writers ever run out of ideas?" Maybe some do, but for me t'ain't so. It seems the more I exercise the ole cerebral muscles, the more easily plotlines form and beg to be committed to paper or hard-drive. If I'm really on my game writing a piece, the kernels for three more stories may hit me in the process of developing my current one.

And sometimes...sometimes my brain doesn't quite shut down when I go to bed after a solid block of writing. Once the idea pump has been primed, it often continues dribbling as I sleep, and those salient ideas spill over into my dreams. They're usually quite disturbing. And I love every one of them.

Now you're probably already guessing where this is going, and if you guessed "The Gates of Emile Plimpkin" started life as a dream, you'd be right. In the bleak and foggy beginnings of slumber one October night, I saw in my mind's eye the image of a dwarf, silhouetted in the moonlight and rocking from side to side. It was an inspiring vision, which immediately jarred me awake. Intuitively, I knew things about this dwarf. He was dangerous, not to be trusted, a murderer. I also recall, as I tried to doze off again, thinking, "Gate. This has something to do with a gate."

Sunday morning I put off whatever other project I was working on and started writing this new crazy thing. The name of the decidedly meek and reluctant hero hit me almost immediately. I don't know why, but Emile Plimpkin had to be the name. And the villain's name came unbidden with similar ease. The rest sort of fell into place. Elements crowded in, demanding to be added to this strange new stew: Stumpy Joe's backstory, his method of murder by poison, Emile's emerging talent, a pinch of necrophilia for extra kick, Emile's mysterious walking stick.

Now about that walking stick... originally, I had put the two opposing faces on it for no other reason than I thought that detail would be a cool visual. But then I decided to look up what that two faced image of Janus represented—you know, because there might be more stuff I could work in. Imagine my shock upon learning Janus is the patron god of...wait for it..."gates and doorways!" Gooseflesh prickled my arms. I had just struck a very rich vein of material here, and purely by accident!

Or was it by accident? I'm sure I must have heard or read this information about Janus at some point before in my life (how could I not have?), and that knowledge had been tucked away in some dusty corner of my brain, waiting until the day its status turned from inane tidbit to useful prompt. Yes, surely my subconscious nudged me in the right direction during my writing process. While I was busy constructing sentences, my subconscious was lending a hand by suggesting dots that might be connected.

To sum up, in many ways the origins of the story mirror the story itself. This is a tale about dream travel, which was inspired by a dream, and my subconscious guided me along in much the same way the old god Janus guides Emile.

Weird, eh? Yeah, I thought so, too.

Hopefully you've enjoyed the story, and if you did, give me a shout on Facebook or shoot me an email. Especially if you'd like to see more of Emile. Like his friend, the parson, I suspect his adventures have only just begun. And I've been dreaming again...

Secondary note pertinent to storytelling: As of this writing, I've learned I'll be sharing TOC space with the one and only purveyor of dark fantasy and science fiction, Mr. William F. Nolan.

I happened to meet Mr. Nolan at Pulpfest in Columbus, Ohio, a couple of years back, and he gave me, a budding writer, some sage advice I've carried in my head ever since.

"You've got to make your fiction compelling," he said. So true. Basically, it boils down to this, your prose can sing, your research may be thorough, and your manuscript free of typos, but if readers don't give a damn about what happens, it's all over. Fundamentally, the difference between a good story and a bad story is the tale's ability to command an audience's attention. What makes us read on? According to Nolan, if there are questions which must be answered, and if we care about the characters, we'll want to be with them when they solve that mystery, destroy that mother ship, save the girl. If there is tension, we want to be there to see things through to their resolution. Tell a joke, we'll wait for the punch line. I'll add my two cents to this and say there is a psychology within the writer-reader relationship. But it's more than playing with the reader. That would be one-sided and selfish. What we do is open the engine up full throttle and suggest everyone come along for a little joy ride. Fiction is best when it's shared, after all.

I've thought a great deal about Nolan's brief but exceptionally poignant observation about storytelling and wanted to share the sentiment with other would-be writers.

Make it compelling.

Three simple words. Words to live by.

–*S. Clayton Rhodes*

"Smoking, The Old Sergeant Remembers 30 Mins Past Ceasefire"

The poem—or the idea of it, at least—has haunted me for years, ever since I had a difficult discussion in a smoke-filled room about war crimes with a former Major. The Major was one of the residents in the retirement home where I worked for many years. The smoke in the Major's room was usually so thick, I could hear the TV playing in the background but I couldn't always see it. It's worth noting that the Major himself was a pilot, not an infantryman. To end on a humorous side note: one thing that always stuck with me about his room was a picture of a WWI plane

that he had crash-landed in the snow after a failed landing. The plane was intact for the most part, except for the nose which was crushed, and it stood erect in the snow, with the Major standing beside it with a grin.

–*Dominik Parisien*

"The Horror That Et My Pap—and Other Swamp Stuff"

I wrote this little sketch after reading my good friend Joe R. Lansdale's last book, *Edge of Dark Water*. It was so rich with dialect and atmosphere I felt compelled to jot this down. I hope people will like it.

–*William F. Nolan*

"Shall I Whisper to You of Moonlight, of Sorrow, of Pieces of Us?"

I'm not a plotter and usually have only a vague idea of where a story is going to go when I write the first sentence. When I started "Shall I Whisper to You of Moonlight, of Sorrow, of Pieces of Us?" I thought it was about a stalker, but as the story unfolded, I realized that wasn't precisely the case.

I told the story as it came to me, flitting back and forth in time, and, once I reached the end, I wasn't sure if the narrator's grief created the ghost, or if the ghost was sustaining (and prolonging) the main character's grief because of its own inability to say goodbye, or if perhaps the ghost was a figment of imagination born of the narrator's grief. It would've been easy to clarify either way, but I opted to leave it as is and let the readers decide for themselves.

–Damien Angelica Walters

"The Long Road"

Shortly before I discovered I was pregnant with my first child, I had a dream. In my dream, I was walking a long dirt road with marshland surrounding both sides. Even in the dream, I was confused. The marshland of South Carolina was the land of my grandmother. My land is filled with pine trees and pollen, but whenever I smell that sickening mixture of salt and decay, there are pieces of my soul that settle deep into that smell.

So I was walking this road, and the smell was all around me. Ahead of me, my husband walked, but his movements were jerky, as if each step was a deliberate process, a forced bending of the knee, the foot purposefully pressed in the dust.

I called to him over and over, my throat went hoarse and bloody with the force of it, but he wouldn't turn around, wouldn't acknowledge why we were walking on this road. And I was afraid.

There was something moving in the water, and somehow I knew that whatever was in that water had taken my husband away, and I would be left alone on that awful road, forever walking, forever lost in that fetid smell.

It was the aloneness that I feared most. That I would be on this road for the rest of my life, moving toward some unfixed point with no one to guide, to help, to offer love or comfort.

This was a fear that I'd been having in waking life. I'd lost two babies in a year before that dream. Feared that my body was broken, that I would be alone and in pieces despite my husband's reassurances that he was right here with me.

And so the story started in the marsh with Danny boy making the decision to run, to run away from the very land that defined him. But it always came back to that aloneness, to that feeling of not being able to escape, of not being able to get off of that long road.

Two days after finishing the first draft, I found out I was pregnant again. It's a boy.

–Kristi DeMeester

"Thing In a Bag"

I'm an old-fashioned horror movie fan. I'll watch any old creature-feature with rapt attention—whether the creature is a stuntman in fish prosthetics, a rear-projected spider blown up a hundred times, or a quivering blob of pink silicon jelly. I go absolutely nuts for stop-motion, and I still think Willis O'Brien and Ray Harryhausen ought never to have gone a day without work.

I'll watch anything with Vincent Price, or anything directed by Roger Corman. I've spent hours on YouTube just watching the trailers to William Castle flicks. And I have annual traditions built around the movies of Val Lewton. (Sorry, Universal fans, but it's a fact that Boris Karloff did his best work for RKO.) I get legitimate chills from *Carnival of Souls* and *The Fly* and *The Innocents*.

Among my own stories, "Thing In a Bag" was my first creature-feature. I wrote it years ago as a gift for a friend of mine who's also a horror movie buff—though she goes for the REALLY scary stuff. (Hi, Kate!) The story takes the nervous criminal on the run from *Psycho*, the digestive ooze from *The Blob*, the sinister shape-shifting from *Invasion of the Body Snatchers*, and the nasty twist ending from *The Twilight Zone*. It's no wonder that when I dug it up again recently, I still loved every word of it.

Not being the brightest writer on the planet, I kept sending this story to science-fiction magazines. They kept writing back and saying, "You know, this is really a horror story." After a few of those, I finally got the message and sent it to *Shock Totem*, and was delighted to find that I'm not the only modern horror fan who still loves these old-fashioned chills.

–M. Bennardo

SILENT Q DESIGN

Silent Q Design was founded in Montreal in 2006 by **Mikio Murakami.**
Melding together the use of both realistic templates and surreal imagery,
Mikio's artistry proves, at first glance, that a passion for art still is alive,
and that no musician, magazine, or venue should suffer from the same
bland designs that have been re-hashed over and over.

Mikio's work has been commissioned both locally and internationally, by
bands such as **Redemption, Synastry, Starkweather,** and **Epocholypse.**
Shock Totem #3 was his first book design project.

For more info, visit **www.silentqdesign.net.**

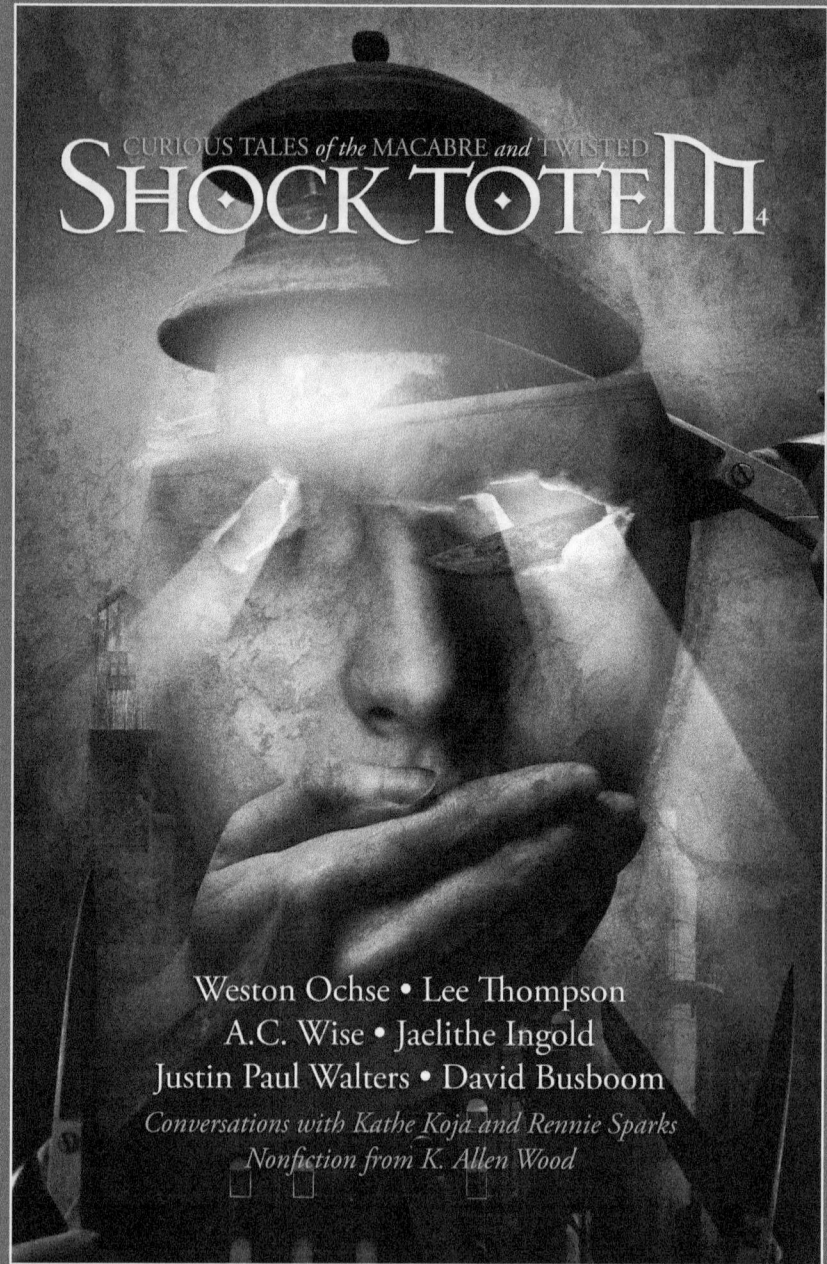

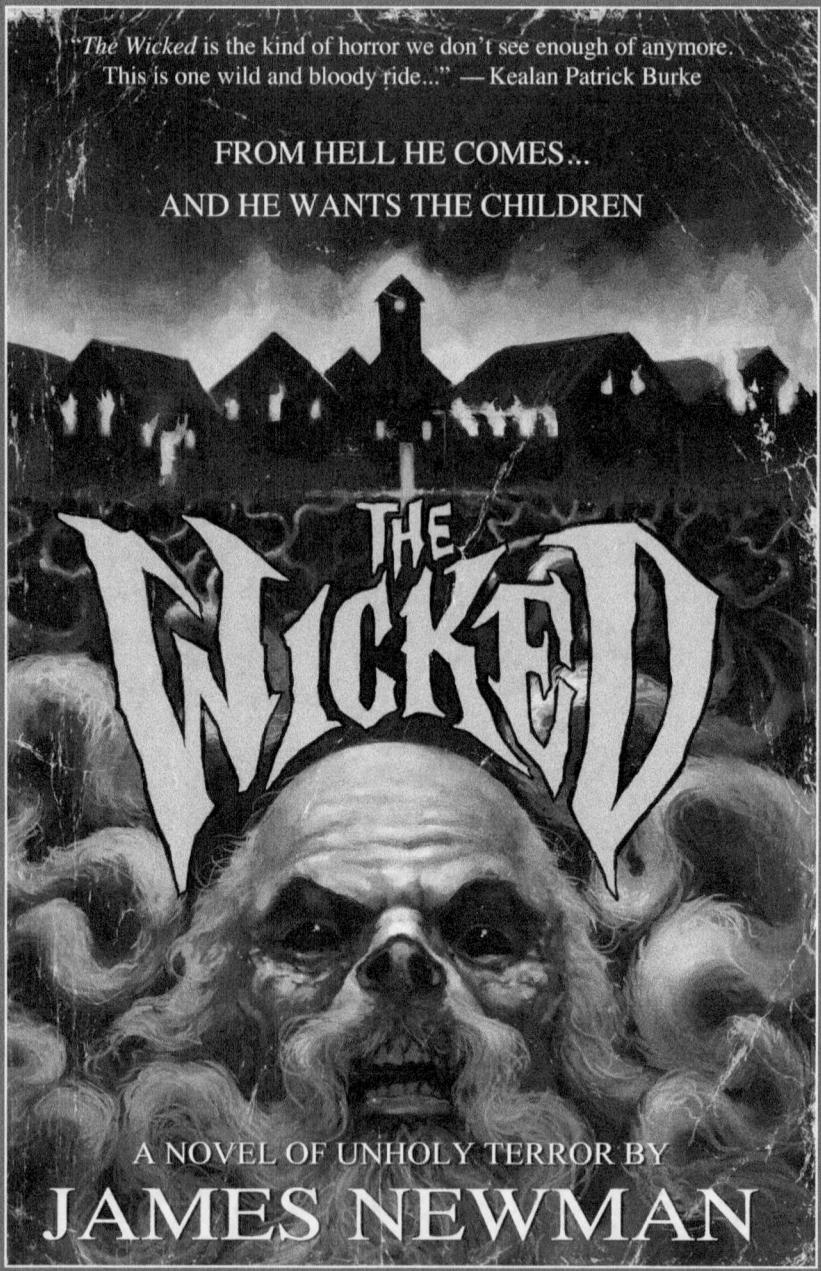

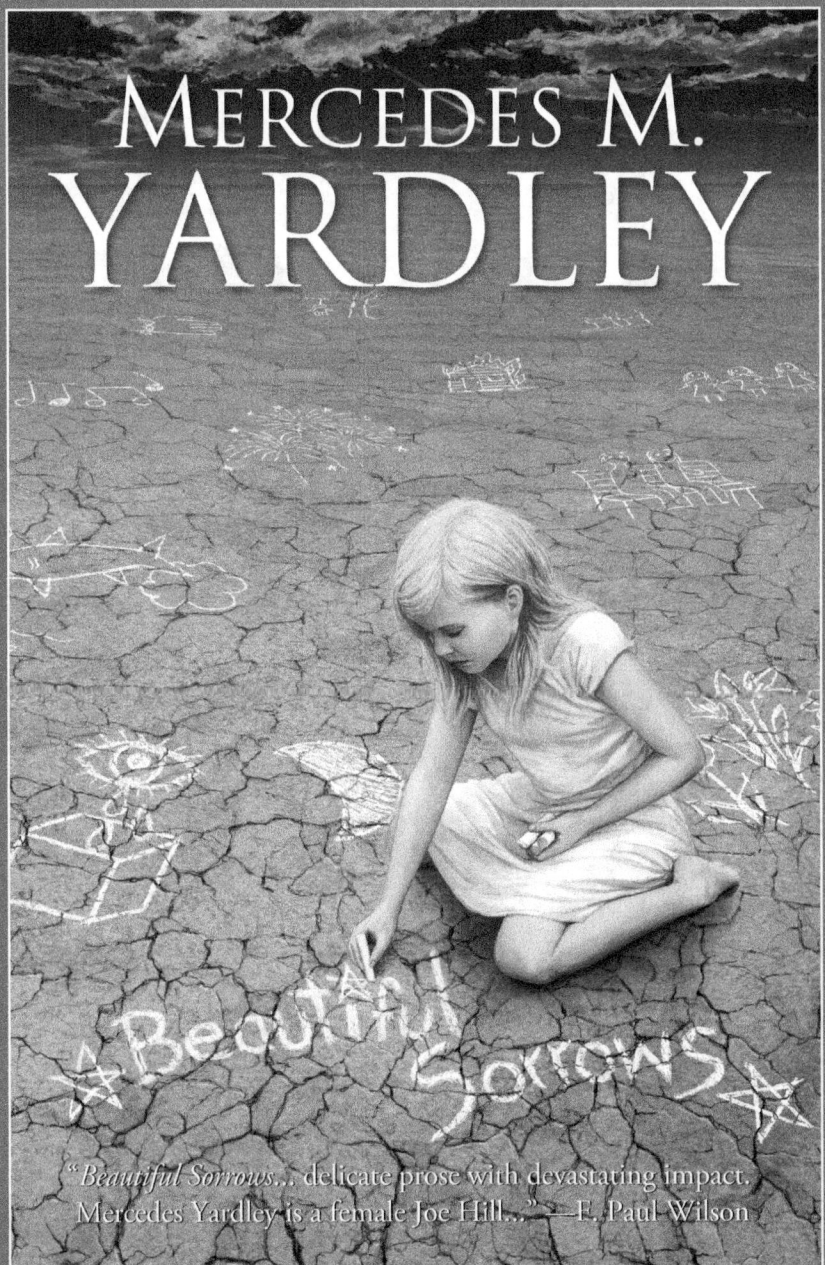

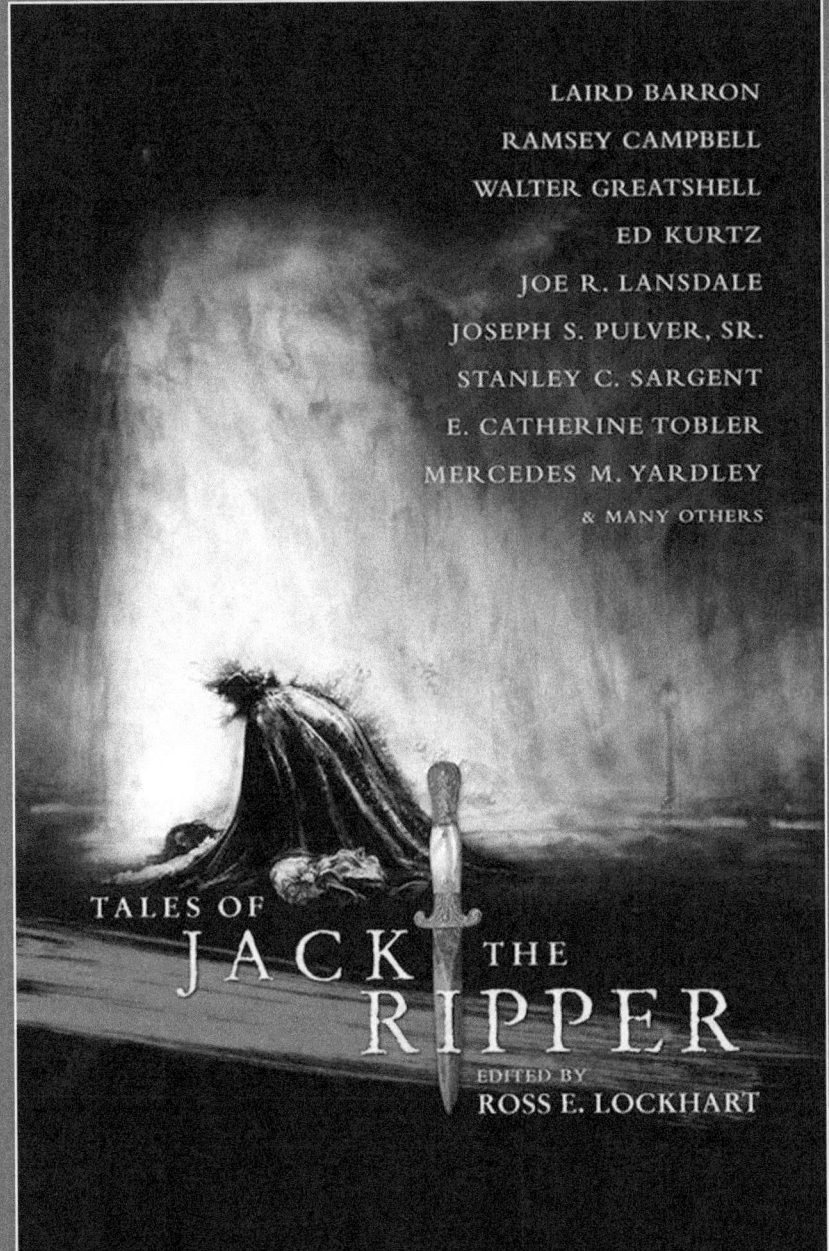

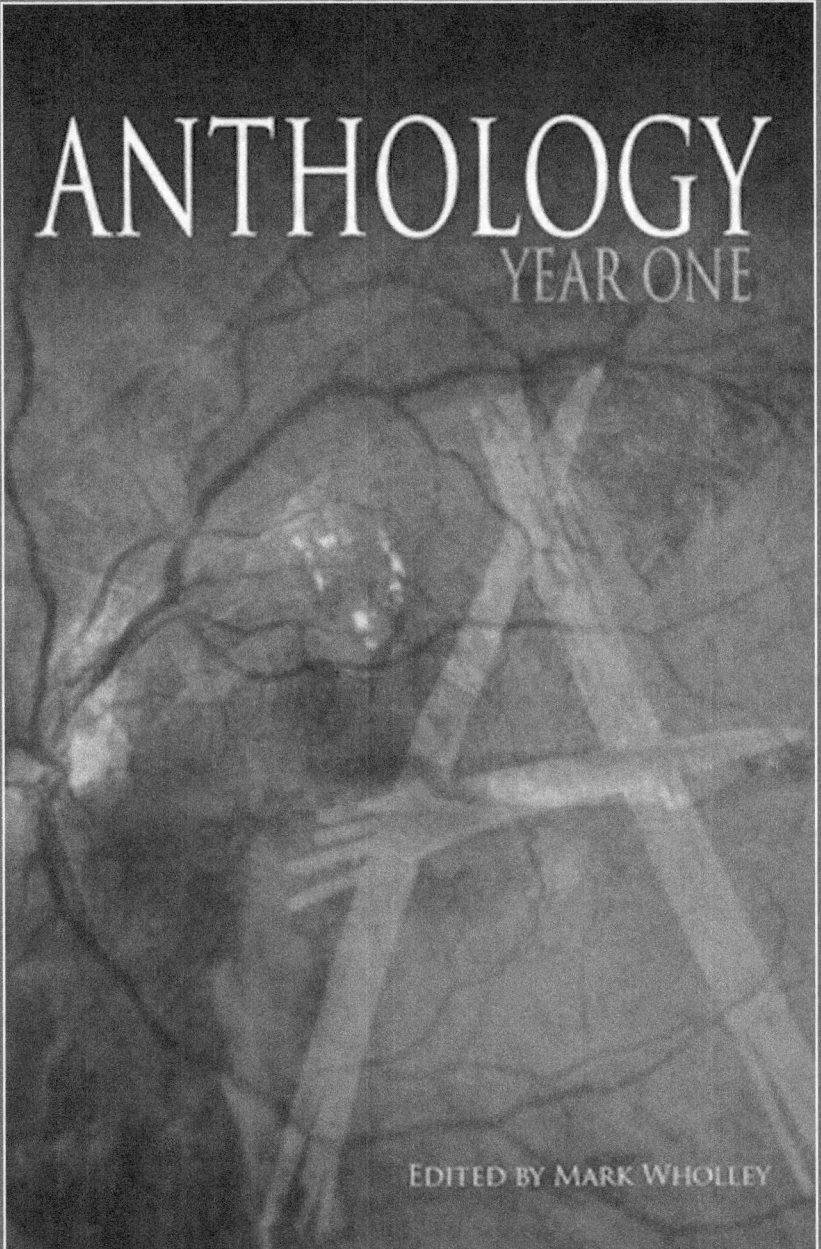

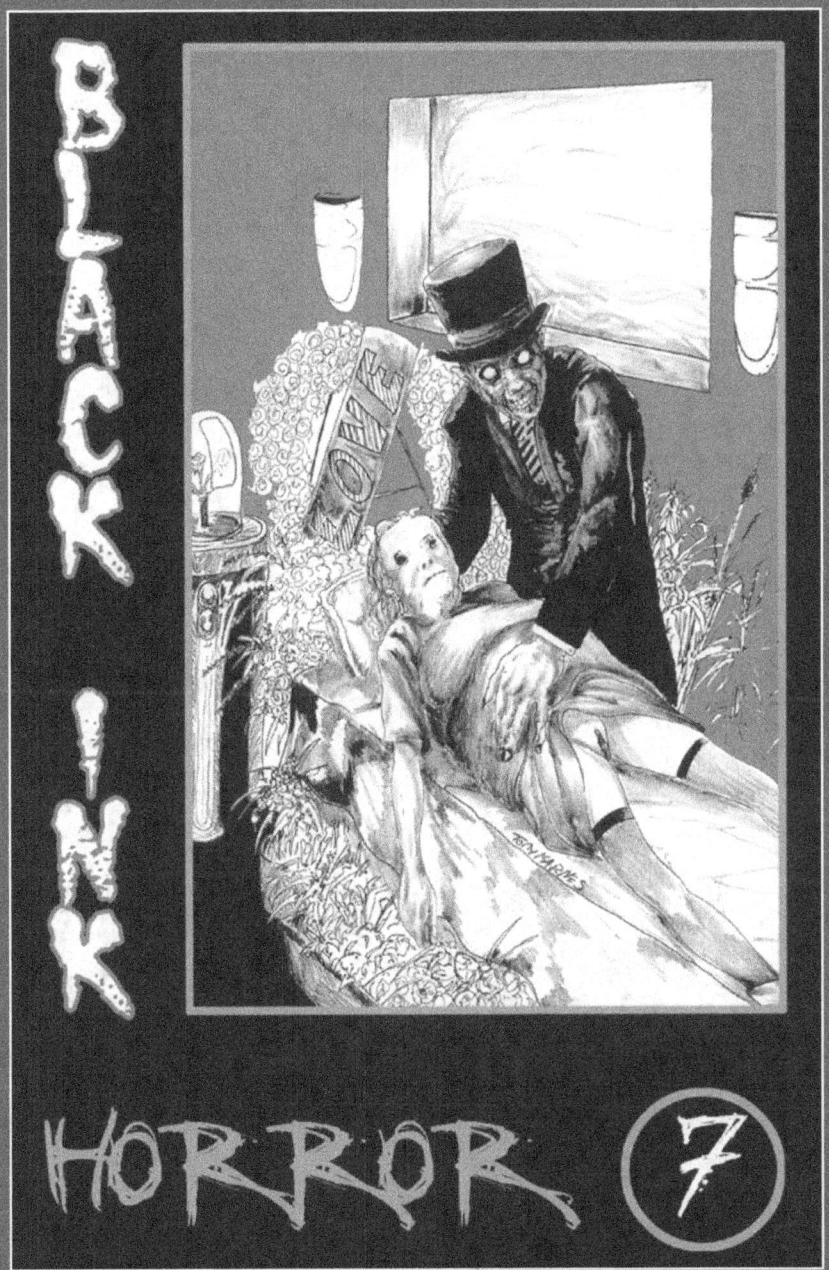

52 STITCHES
HORROR STORIES

edited by Aaron Polson

FIND US ONLINE

http://www.shocktotem.com
http://www.twitter.com/shocktotem
http://www.facebook.com/shocktotem
http://www.youtube.com/shocktotemmag

SHOCK TOTEM SUBMISSION GUIDELINES

What We Want: We consider original, unpublished stories within the confines of dark fantasy and horror—mystery, suspense, supernatural, morbid humor, fantasy, etc. Stories must have a clear horror element.

We are interested in tightly woven flash fiction, 1,000 words or less, and microfiction, 200 words or less.

We are interested in dark poetry on a limited basis.

We want well-researched and emotionally compelling nonfiction about real horrors—disease, poverty, addiction, etc. We will also consider work on other, relative subjects within the confines of dark fantasy and horror.

What We Do Not Want: We're not interested in hard science fiction, epic fantasy (swords and sorcery), splatterporn (blood and guts and little more), or clichéd plots. Clichéd *themes* are okay. No fan fiction.

What We Will Consider: Reprints not published within the last 12 months. Author must retain all applicable rights.

Average Response Time: 2 months.

Payment Rates: We pay 5 cents per word for original, unpublished fiction. We pay 2 cents per word for reprints. There is a $250 cap on all accepted pieces.

Rights: For previously unpublished work we claim First North American Serial Rights and First Electronic World Rights (not to include Internet use) for a period of one year. After which all rights revert to the author.

For previously published work we claim Exclusive Reprint Rights and Exclusive Electronic World Reprint Rights (not to include Internet use) for a period of six months. After which all rights revert to the author.

For more detailed information, please visit us at
www.shocktotem.com

www.ingramcontent.com/pod-product-compliance
Lightning Source LLC
Chambersburg PA
CBHW060633130626
46555CB00002B/789